THE DRAGON RIDER'S DAUGHTER

SUZANNE G. ROGERS

IDUNN COURT PUBLISHING

CONTENTS

Idunn Court Publishing
7 Ramshorn Court
Savannah, GA 31411

First published as *Minna and the Valentine* by Astraea Press, February 2012
Published in the United States of America
Cover Design: Suzanne G. Rogers

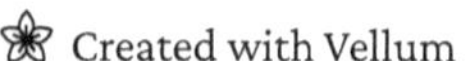 Created with Vellum

CHAPTER I

WICKED MAGIC

When twelve-year-old Evan Valentine and his mother arrived at the Aldesbury Magic Academy, he was awed by its majestic Gothic-style buildings and aura of historical importance. Just passing through the tall wrought iron gates at the entrance of the school made the hair on his forearms stand on end. As they mounted the steps to the main hall, he rolled up his sleeve to show his gooseflesh to his mother.

"Look! I'm not even cold."

She nodded. "It's the energy here that's giving you goose bumps. I'm not particularly magical and even I can feel it."

As they moved down the marble-tiled hall toward the admissions office, he tried to ignore the titters and dismissive glances directed his way. The students wore uniforms, of course, but their attitude of arrogance and entitlement was intimidating. He tugged the too-short cuffs of his freshly laundered shirt as far down on his wrists as possible, but his efforts to lengthen them were fruitless. Furthermore, nothing could conceal his worn boots, the darned knee of his corduroy pants, or the dreadful haircut his mother had given him in the bathroom at home.

Mrs. Valentine noticed him fidgeting with his clothes. "Don't fret, lad. We may be poor, but our hearts are in the right place."

Although her words were meant to be comforting, Evan's heart sank even lower than before. If his mother had noticed he was the object of amusement, he must look worse than he thought. His confidence plummeted, and he began to regret coming with every fiber of his being.

Just outside the frosted glass doors of the office, he grabbed his mother's sleeve.

"Maybe this isn't such a good idea."

"Why not?" She regarded him with solemn blue eyes. "We have an appointment."

He leaned in to whisper, "We can't pay the tuition. Even if I'm offered a full scholarship, we can't even afford the uniforms."

"Uniforms can be purchased secondhand." She patted his cheek and gave him an encouraging smile. "First, we must prove you have the ability to study magic."

Once they'd entered the office, his mother waved him toward a row of chairs. "Have a seat until the examiner calls your name."

He frowned. "Where are you going?"

"Not far. I'm just going to check in with the secretary, give her my financial aid form, and meet with the admissions counselor."

Evan ambled toward an empty chair, sank into it, and glanced around the room. Despite his embarrassment about his shabby appearance, he was excited to be at the school, nevertheless. Could he impress the examiner enough to be offered a full scholarship? Never in his wildest dreams had he imagined pursuing a magical education...until his homeroom teacher, Mrs. Allifax, witnessed him transform a pile of pencil shavings into a miniature tornado and send it swirling into the school bully's lunch. Instead of writing him up for an infraction, she'd given Evan an application to the Academy.

What if he didn't have the right stuff to qualify? Or maybe the examiners were expecting him to have had a more formal education in the magical arts. Evan sucked in a deep breath and blew it out slowly. Either way, it was too late to back out now. To distract himself from the ball of nerves roiling his stomach, he brought out one of the folding papers he almost always kept in his pocket and began to fashion a dragon. The Dragon National Championship was the following day—a Saturday—and dragons had been on his mind. Since his mother didn't own a vidscreen, he planned to watch the race at the local pub with Uncle Joe.

Evan was so consumed by the task at hand, he didn't take heed of anything until a long caramel-colored braid swung into his peripheral vision. When he glanced up, his mouth went dry. The prettiest girl he'd ever seen was sitting next to him and staring at his handiwork. She was clad in a plaid kilt, shiny patent-leather shoes, and a dainty white blouse, and her braid was tied on the end with a pink ribbon. The girl was so close, he could smell the perfumed soap lingering on her skin. The hair on his forearms stood on end again, just as she giggled and rubbed her own bare forearms.

"Are you giving me goose bumps?"

He shook his head. "Not on purpose."

Although he wanted to keep staring into the girl's hazel eyes, he forced his attention back to the last few folds of his paper. Afterward, he held the finished creation out on the palm of his hand.

"Can you tell what it is?"

"Of course." She wriggled in excitement. "A dragon!"

He was relieved she hadn't thought it was a bird. "Yeah."

"What's it for?"

"It doesn't have any purpose, really." He shrugged. "I fold paper when I'm nervous." Immediately, he wished he'd bitten his tongue. Why couldn't he have played it cool?

She fixed him with her gaze. "Are you nervous about the evaluation?"

"A bit. You?"

"Terrified." She gulped. "I wish I knew what the examiner was going to ask."

"I expect you'll do okay, whatever it is." His gaze rested on the gold charm bracelet fastened around her wrist, featuring various breeds of dragons. "You like dragons?"

"I adore them. My father's a dragon jockey and we own a dragon ranch. He lets me break in the young ones when they're ready to fly."

The girl suddenly seemed to take on a golden sheen of glamour, and Evan became tongue-tied. He finally managed a lame, "T-That's really something."

What could he do to impress her? Although he didn't know much formal magic yet, he knew how to do a few things without having been taught. His paper dragon took off and flew around in a circle, flapping its tiny paper wings.

"How marvelous!" The girl gaped. "You're so clever."

"Hold out your hand, palm up." When she stuck out her hand, the dragon landed on her dainty palm and folded its wings at its side. "Keep it, if you want. For luck."

She beamed. "Thank you!"

To his utter shock, she jumped up to deposit a kiss on his cheek. "For luck."

Although his cheeks grew warm from embarrassment, he

couldn't stop a foolish grin from spreading across his face. "Thanks."

"Evan?" A man with a clipboard stood next to the secretary's desk, beckoning to him. "We're ready for you now."

He nodded and got to his feet. "Yes, sir."

"Bye!" The girl gave Evan a little wave. "My name's Minna Westerfield. Maybe we'll be in the same class next year."

Westerfield? A shock ran through him at the realization she must be Wynn Westerfield's daughter.

"Maybe." He paused. "I-I hope so."

He threw back his shoulders and strode toward the waiting examiner, feeling far more confident than he had before. After all, the very pretty daughter of a famous dragon jockey had just given him a kiss for luck.

MINNA PRACTICALLY SKIPPED with joy as she left Aldesbury Magic Academy with her mother.

"And at the end of the evaluation, Mr. Howell asked me to do something with the blocks he'd never seen before. I turned them into ice cubes. Well, they weren't *really* ice, but they looked that way. He said it was an inspired choice." Her smile slipped. "Of course, maybe everyone turns the blocks to ice and he was just being kind to me." Her shoulders slumped. "The more I think about it, it was stupidly obvious, and I should have done something far more clever. Evan probably enchanted his blocks to float to the ceiling."

"Evan?"

"The boy who went in just before me." She produced the paper dragon from her pocket, making sure to hold it carefully so it wouldn't crease or tear. "He made this dragon fly, can you believe it? He's so talented."

"Yes indeed, but I'm certain what you did was impressive as well."

"How do you know? We don't hear the results for a week."

"The examiner made sure to catch my eye after your evaluation. He gave me a wink and a nod, so I'm sure you did splendidly."

"I'm not sure at all." She returned the dragon to her pocket. "Mr. Howell could be a fan of Papa's. I don't want to be given special consideration because of my father."

"Certainly not, but no child would be admitted to the school unless he or she had the ability to succeed." The woman smiled. "You're exceptionally gifted, Minna. Don't ever doubt it."

In a rush of gratitude, Minna gave her mother a hug. "You always say the right thing."

Once they left the school grounds, Nancy Westerfield hailed a taxi to take them back to the Aldesbury Dragon Park. As they settled in for the drive across town, Minna's mother leaned forward to catch the driver's attention. "We're under a bit of a time constraint."

"Yes, ma'am." The vehicle surged forward.

Minna frowned. "I hope we aren't too late to watch Papa qualify?"

"As long as we don't hit traffic, we'll be right on time."

"Good. I can hardly wait to tell him about my evaluation! When he realizes how well I did, surely he'll see the Academy is the perfect place for me."

Her mother frowned. "Um...let's not say anything to him about the school just now. With the race tomorrow, he has a lot on his mind."

Minna gave her a worried glance. "You don't think he'll be angry, do you?"

"N-Not exactly, but it's best to wait until we receive a letter offering you admission. If I have something specific to show him, he'll look upon the school more favorably."

"Why does Papa dislike magic so much?"

Nancy tweaked Minna's braid. "Your father likes to rely on things he can control."

"Like his dragon, Crucible?"

"Exactly."

Minna recalled her delight when the paper dragon flew around the admissions office. "I hope Evan and I are both admitted to the school, so I'll know one other person."

"Don't get your hopes up. He might be admitted, but I don't think he'll be able to attend." Nancy's eyes reflected compassion. "From the way he and his mother were dressed, they didn't appear to have much money."

"I know." She frowned. "It's unfair to turn away someone like Evan just because of money."

"It does seem unfair, but a large school like Aldesbury Magic Academy has to have sufficient funds to keep running. Upkeep of the buildings and grounds costs a tremendous amount, and then there are the salaries for the faculty and administrators to consider."

"Well, I hope Evan finds a way to pay the tuition."

"I'll keep my fingers crossed for him." Nancy smiled. "Don't worry overmuch about it. If the lad's gifted, his mother will probably arrange for him to study magic, even if it's on his own. I know that's what I'd do for you if our family lost our money."

"Papa would prefer magic didn't exist, I think." Minna sighed. "Won't he wonder where we went today?"

"He's probably been too busy to notice our absence, but if he asks, we'll say we went to visit Aunt Bettina."

Minna grimaced. "I like Aunt Bettina, but she's a little scary."

Her mother laughed. "Everyone finds your great-aunt a bit intimidating, but that's why she's the perfect alibi. Nobody dares question her."

"I don't like telling lies, even white ones." She wrinkled her nose. "I hope Papa doesn't ask where we've been."

"Maybe he won't. His sponsors are giving him a press party this afternoon, and he's expected to give interviews. I suspect he'll have too many distractions to wonder how we spent our morning."

Minna rolled her eyes. "It's so funny people think of him as a celebrity. To me, he's just Papa."

Her mother laughed. "To me, he's just the most wonderful man I've ever known. I'm terribly proud of him."

Evan's delight overflowed when his mother took him into an ice cream counter after his evaluation. While Mrs. Valentine nursed a cup of coffee, he dug his spoon into a banana split with gusto, licking whipped cream, chopped nuts, and thick hot fudge sauce from his spoon with every mouthful of delectable ice cream.

He glanced up from the rare treat with a smile of gratitude. "This is great."

"I thought you should have a reward before we go home."

"I'm sorry you had to take the day off from work."

"I'm not." She ruffled his hair affectionately. "I've not taken a day off from the bakery since I began working there, so I think I'm entitled. Besides which, piping icing on cupcakes can be done by anyone else at the shop."

He grinned. "Maybe I'll learn some spells to help you with your work."

Mrs. Valentine paused before taking a sip of coffee. "Maybe so."

The vidscreen mounted on the wall competed with the ice cream for Evan's attention. The news was showing vidclips of the qualifying races at Aldesbury Dragon Park. Dragons of every breed whizzed past the camera while sunlight reflected off their colorful scales. The jockeys, clad in racing silks, sat just above their dragons' shoulders, in custom-made leather saddles. The riders—men known for their strength and athletic prowess—were bent low against their mounts' massive necks. The spectacle was a thing of beauty and grace, and Evan could scarcely look away.

His mother followed his gaze. "Dragon jockeys must have nerves and muscles of steel to control those enormous beasts. Are you looking forward to watching the race tomorrow?"

"Of course!" Evan pulled a cherry off its stem with his teeth and sucked the sweet juice from the fruit. "You know that girl I met today—Minna? Her father's Wynn Westerfield."

"He is?" Mrs. Valentine's sigh was almost girlish. "I must admit, Wynn Westerfield is terribly handsome. I saw him in person a few years ago, signing posters. I wish I could have bought one for you."

"If I'd known Minna was related to him, I probably would've been too nervous to talk to her."

"I don't blame you. She *was* a very pretty girl."

"Argh." Evan stuck out his tongue, as if in disgust. "I didn't notice."

His mother chuckled. "No, of course not." She sipped her coffee. "You seemed pleased with your evaluation."

"Mr. Howell asked me to do something with the blocks he hadn't seen before, so I transformed them into balls. You should have seen his face when they rolled off the edge of the table!"

"Did you leave them that way?"

"No, they turned back into blocks as soon as they fell." Evan grinned and twisted back and forth on his swivel stool, despite a glance of disapproval from the attendant. "After Mr. Howell made some notes, he said letters of decision would be going out in about a week."

"Er...I spoke with the admissions counselor while you were being evaluated, to explain our financial situation." Mrs. Valentine averted her eyes. "The counselor was very kind, but she let me know the school doesn't award full scholarships."

"Oh." The ice cream in Evan's stomach turned sour. "Well... that's no different than I'd thought."

"The results of your evaluation will determine the level of your scholarship, if any." She frowned. "Whatever the amount, it won't defray the tuition enough to make a difference."

"Can Uncle Joe help?" Even as the question left his lips, he knew the answer.

"I'm sure my brother would love to help, but with a new baby on the way, he and Ivy have nothing to spare." His mother's tone was carefully neutral, but the muscles around her mouth were tight. "I'm sorry, sweetheart. I'm afraid I've raised your hopes for nothing."

He feigned indifference. "It wasn't for nothing. If I'm offered a place at the school, at least I'll know I was good enough, right? And if I don't get in, I won't have any regrets about not trying." Evan nudged the heavy glass bowl toward his mother. "Do you want some ice cream?"

"No, it's yours." Her smile was sad. "Maybe you can check out some books on magic from the library."

Despite the fact he was devastated, Evan would do anything to ease his mother's pain.

"Sure, there's a whole shelf devoted to magic at the library."

"That's the spirit. Only…I'd keep your hobby to yourself. People who aren't magical don't usually like wizards."

"I've noticed."

With that, the full disappointment of the day finally sank in, and he finished his ice cream without tasting it. Buoyed by his evaluation, he'd allowed himself to hope his life would change for the better. If he could attend the Academy, he'd go to school alongside kids with real talent and magical futures. He'd planned to study magic harder than he'd ever studied anything before and hopefully graduate with honors. Certainly, nobody would snicker or poke fun at an accomplished wizard…even one whose father had drunk himself into an early grave. Without money to pay the tuition, however, his daydreams would come to nothing.

As more dragons flashed across the vidscreen, he was reminded of Minna Westerfield. What must it be like to be the child of a celebrity and live a charmed existence? Her father was practically a national hero and judging by her clothes and jewelry, she had all the money she needed. If Evan had the chance to swap his lot in life for hers, he'd do it in a heartbeat. The way things stood now, however, he'd have to put magic aside and learn a proper trade.

Evan stared, unseeing, into space as his emotions spiraled downward. *This must be what it feels like when a dream dies.* He swallowed hard and slid from his stool.

"Come on, Mother. Let's go home."

THE FOLLOWING AFTERNOON, Evan and his uncle walked to the pub around the corner from their house to watch the Dragon National Championship on the huge vidscreen. The watering hole was crammed full of good-natured fans who bickered with one another on who would win the race.

With a basket of salted in-shell peanuts at hand and a glass of lemonade, Evan enjoyed the majestic opening ceremony, especially when a professional demonstration team of synchronized dragon riders flew fantastic maneuvers over the enormous semi-circular stadium. After a glamorous and well-endowed vocalist sang the national anthem of Ceresland, jockeys flew their mounts into position. A close-up shot of Wynn Westerfield made the most of his handsome face, and several of the ladies in the pub trilled with appreciation.

Joe snickered. "There you go, lad. Become a dragon jockey and you'll have all the feminine admiration you can handle."

Since his uncle didn't yet know about Evan's visit to the Academy, he ventured a joke.

"I'd love to ride a dragon, but I'd rather be a wizard."

"Wizards are overrated, in my humble opinion. Magical types sometimes come to sticky ends, you see. Best to stay out of trouble and learn to work with your hands like I do." His uncle picked up a bar napkin. "Hey, remember the trick I showed you?"

As Evan watched, Joe folded the thin paper into the shape of a puppy. A female waitress passing by pounced on it right away. "Isn't that cute!"

Joe winked at Evan. "See what I mean? I hope you've been practicing."

"Yeah, I have. A little."

His uncle nodded. "You're a good-looking kid. In a couple of years, girls will be falling all over you."

"Not dressed this way, they won't." Evan shrugged.

"Not every woman wants a man with money. I'm proof of that."

Evan cracked open a peanut. "What do you mean?"

"I haven't got more than two pennies to rub together, but Ivy believes in me." He paused. "Don't forget, girls love puppies."

"And dragons."

Although Evan didn't want to contradict his uncle, he couldn't imagine any scenario in which a rich girl like Minna Westerfield would ever agree to marry a poor boy like him—no matter how many puppies or dragons he folded for her entertainment.

Increasingly discouraged, he turned his attention to the vidscreen. Although he was indifferent to Wynn's appearance, he admired the man's athleticism and confident air. In addition, his coppery dragon was the most breathtaking of the lot. The sleek and muscular creature possessed a triangular-shaped head, broad shoulders perfectly situated for a saddle, a magnificent set of wings, and a long tail ending in a sharp point. From the arrogant way Crucible tossed his head and pawed the ground, the glorious animal was evidently aware he was far above his company.

Prince Percival climbed the stairs to a mobile tower adjacent to the track, and Evan leaned forward in anticipation. When His Highness pointed the starting pistol skyward and squeezed the trigger, the subsequent crack made Evan's adrenaline surge. Dragons surged through their gates, and the resulting whoosh of air knocked the hats off people in the lower stands and mussed their hair. The prince's bowler tumbled off his balding head and went sailing across the grass, prompting a mad scramble among his attendants to retrieve it. In short order, the dragons rounded the surface track and then left the main stadium in favor of the winding canyons comprising the course. Cameras were positioned every quarter mile to transmit the action back to the vidscreens in the stadium and worldwide.

Uncle Joe's expression seemed lit from within as he gave Evan a nudge. "Exciting, isn't it?"

Transfixed on the race, Evan could only manage to nod. While the action was underway, a duo of sportscasters offered a running commentary about statistics and style. Evan wasn't surprised to discover the consensus favored Wynn Westerfield and Crucible, but he was only half attending. The incredible spectacle of dragons speeding along the course, hugging the tight turns and brushing up against the canyon walls was far more riveting than any remarks either of the sportscasters could offer. After the first few miles of the race, however, Evan was puzzled. Wynn Westerfield was following the leader instead of taking point. Behind him, the rest of the pack was more evenly spaced out. Would his hero fail to cross the finish line first?

Evan tugged his uncle's sleeve to get his attention. "Is he trying to lose?"

Joe bent his head closer. "What?"

He raised his voice over the cacophony of noise in the pub. "Wynn Westerfield is letting Hank Kelso and Songbird fly in front of him!"

"Of course he is!" Joe grinned. "His strategy is to let Kelso set the pace for now. When Songbird tires at the end, you'll see Westerfield slip past for the win."

One of the patrons overheard. "Don't worry, lad. Westerfield has this in the bag." He lifted his glass of ale, as if in a toast. "I've got a bet riding on it!"

As Evan watched the race unfold, however, his anxiety increased. It didn't seem like the jockey's strategy—if that's what it was—would succeed. What if Crucible tired instead and the rest of the pack overcame him?

The course turned increasingly dangerous at the midpoint, with a series of obstacles, harrowing turns and blind curves that made Evan grit his teeth. He didn't need the sportscasters' commentary to see the prowess of the riders for himself. The treacherous course allowed for no mistakes, and when one of the dragons caught a wingtip on a rocky overhang, the creature careened toward the bottom of the canyon. The unfortunate jockey slid from his saddle, and although a tether prevented him from plummeting to his death, his body dangled midair. The pub breathed a collective sigh of relief when the dragon managed to land, and shortly thereafter a rescue crew arrived to render aid to the jockey.

In the meantime, the championship race surged relentlessly forward. Another series of tricky obstacles, from spiral tunnels to narrow, vertical passageways, required the dragons and their riders to utilize every bit of expertise at their disposal. In the final mile, after the pack passed through a thick sheet of water from a manmade spillway spanning the canyon, the jockeys made their final moves. On a sharp curve, Westerfield and Crucible finally shot past Kelso and Songbird and streaked toward the finish line. The crowd at the pub rose to their feet and erupted in ear-splitting excitement. Awestruck, Evan jumped from his seat and cheered along with the rest.

In the blink of an eye, a brick wall appeared directly in front of Westerfield. With only a hundred yards or so between him and disaster, the jockey maneuvered his dragon into a masterful backflip and brought him to a halt. Unfortunately, Kelso and Birdsong barreled around the curve and flew straight into the team. Birdsong panicked and let out a bellow of dragonfire, even as he attempted to avoid a direct collision by pushing backward with his wings. In the next moment, however, the brick wall disappeared. Kelso and Birdsong flew forward once more, albeit awkwardly. Crucible, blinded by the dragonfire and screaming with pain, flew straight into a canyon wall. He dropped like an anvil with his neck at an odd angle, taking Westerfield with him. The rest of the competitors zoomed past, leaving the downed dragon and jockey for the rescue crew.

A collective gasp went up from the crowd at the pub. Aghast and horrified, Evan felt sick to his stomach. A stunned silence ensued from the onlookers as the sportscasters covered the end of the race. Birdsong, clearly unnerved by the near collision, was unable to pull out a win and came in second.

"That was wicked magic, that was!" The bartender pointed an accusatory finger at the vidscreen. "Some wizard tried to kill Westerfield, sure as I'm standing here!"

Speculation at what had happened swirled throughout the pub, but Evan's thoughts and prayers were for Minna. The day before, he would have given anything to have her life. At the moment, however, he pitied her more than he'd ever pitied anyone. Her father was surely gravely hurt—if not worse—and it looked as if magic was the culprit. Even if Wynn Westerfield survived, her life would never be the same. No, he didn't want to change places with her at all.

CHAPTER 2
GOOSE BUMPS

Over six years later...

The fury of an early summer squall pelted against the windowpanes of her bedroom, making it difficult for Minna Westerfield to concentrate on her secondhand copy of *Advanced Incantations—Level Nine*. As she turned the page, the brittle binding split and she found herself holding two halves of the book.

"Not again!"

Minna squeezed the edges together with her fingers while murmuring a mending spell. The rift closed, as if repaired by an unseen zipper, but the fix was only temporary. She didn't have the funds to replace the book, so she'd simply have to redouble her efforts to learn the spells before the text crumbled permanently. Since the information contained in the textbook was critical to her upcoming wizard's licensing exam, the repair would have to last until then.

A sudden flash of light illuminated the woods outside her windows and the almost instantaneous crack of thunder made her flinch. The storm was overhead now and unleashing its energy with unbridled gusto. Her nerves taut, she drew her curtains closed and wished she had a spell to make the storm pass more quickly. Hopefully, the lightning would miss the house—or her father might return home to a burnt cinder.

As she picked up her textbook, an insistent knocking rattled the front door.

Her eyebrows drew together. "What sort of idiot would be out in a squall?"

She tapped the cover of the book, changing the title to *Tansy Goes on a Hayride*. The disguise matched the Tansy novels stacked on a shelf nearby, all of which were secretly textbooks as well. The chances of anyone discovering her library of magic books were slim, but her caution had become second nature. After shelving the book next to a small paper dragon made of faded red paper, she hastened from her bedroom.

Because she was alone, she took the precaution of grabbing a poker as she passed through the living room. Nothing untoward ever happened in Cardinal Hollow, but the storm had her nerves on edge. Weapon in hand, she answered the door.

Silhouetted against the cloud-filtered daylight, a sodden young stranger stood on the porch with an overcoat bundled in his arms. To her knowledge, she'd never met the unusually handsome man before and he certainly didn't live in town.

She peered at him. "Can I help you?"

"Um…sorry to be a bother, but is this your puppy?" The bundle quivered. "I found him in the road outside your house, a bit worse for wear."

The puppy whined and stuck his black nose out from the folds of the fabric. No more than eight weeks old, he was soaked from the rain and shivering.

Her heart melted. "Oh no, the poor fellow must be lost!"

She leaned the poker against the wall and reached for the

bundle. Everything else forgotten, she carried it inside, snatching up a worn throw blanket from the sofa as she passed by. Once she entered the kitchen, she dropped the wet, bulky coat on the kitchen tiles and wrapped the pup in the soft flannel blanket instead.

"You're all right now, little one." After she cuddled the creature on her lap for a minute or so, his shivering slowed. "That's better, but I imagine you're hungry."

She lowered the puppy to the floor and went to pour him some milk. Before she set the saucer on the floor, she used a spell to warm its contents.

Minna beckoned. "Come on, then."

The bedraggled animal trotted over, leaving miniature muddy paw prints in his wake. His tail wagged with satisfaction as he drank. Minna smiled as she stroked the pup's back and scratched behind his floppy ears.

"A cocker spaniel mix, by the look of you."

Her gaze shifted to the coat splayed out nearby and her eyes widened. She'd forgotten all about the man on the porch!

"Oops. I'll be right back. Wait here."

The front door was still ajar when she returned, and as she opened it wider, gooseflesh rose on her arms. Was she reacting to the static electricity released by the lightning? On the porch, the young man was pacing with his hands jammed into his trouser pockets and his shoulders hunched against the cold. Although looks could be deceiving, he didn't appear to pose any danger. If he'd meant her any harm, he certainly could have entered the house while she'd tended to the lost creature.

"I've given the dog a saucer of warm milk and he's stopped shivering. Would you like to come inside for a little while to warm up?"

"I don't want to impose." Despite his words, he glanced

longingly into the house. "Um...if I could have my coat back, I'll be on my way."

The sky lit up with another fierce streak of lightning, and Minna had to raise her voice to be heard over the subsequent peal of thunder.

"Are you out of your senses? You can't walk around in the midst of a lightning storm!" She stepped back to let him by. "Come in."

A ghost of a smile lit the man's lips, which were tinged blue with cold. "Thanks."

To her surprise, he murmured a spell before stepping over the threshold. As he spoke, his trousers and long-sleeved white shirt rid themselves of moisture and mud, and his wet hair sprang up into crisp golden waves.

He held her gaze. "Is something wrong?"

"No, of course not." Minna's cheeks warmed with embarrassment at having been caught staring, and she cast about for an excuse. "We don't get too many wizards around here."

He frowned. "I hope you don't mind."

"No." She shook her head. "I'm not afraid of magic."

"I'm glad."

The man passed into the house, mere inches away, leaving a whiff of aftershave in his wake. The downy hair on Minna's forearms rose again, and it made her shiver. Nevertheless, his smile seemed to warm her.

"Brr, it's cold outside," she said.

"Are squalls very unusual in Cardinal Hollow this time of year?"

"We moved here only four years ago, but the summers have been quite mild until now." Minna shut the door, uncomfortably aware she was clad in old socks, droopy knit leggings, and an oversized flannel shirt her father had discarded years ago. She hastily rolled her sleeves up, hoping it would give her a neater appearance. "Erm...would you care for a cup of coffee or tea? Maybe some hot chocolate?"

"Anything hot, actually, if it's not too much trouble."

"None at all. Why don't you throw a log on the fire and, er, make yourself at home? There are matches on the mantle, and kindling in the basket on the hearth."

Minna bumped into a chair as she turned and then nearly tripped over the puppy as he scampered under her feet.

"What are you doing, little beast? I thought I told you to stay put."

Feeling suddenly clumsy and awkward under the strange man's scrutiny, she scooped the puppy into her arms and carried him into the kitchen. While a pot of hot chocolate warmed on the stove, she snatched the discarded coat from the floor before her guest had the opportunity to notice where she'd left it. The expensive cashmere was wet and dirty—as if it had been dragged through the mud—so she cast a spell to clean it. In the next moment, the camel fabric was pristine again.

"My coat is filthy, I'm afraid." The man appeared in the doorway of the kitchen. "I used it to catch the puppy, but he didn't want to be caught."

Minna bit her lip. "Oh, it *was* a bit dirty but I brushed it off with a cloth." She thrust the coat at him. "It's fine now."

"Really?" He peered at the garment with a puzzled expression. "So it is. I could have sworn it needed a deep cleaning spell."

"Not so much." She pointed to a coat rack on the wall. "You can hang it up on one of those hooks if you like."

"Thanks. My name is Valentine, by the way. Evan Valentine."

"Minna Westerfield."

As he hung his coat on the closest hook within reach, she

couldn't help but admire the man's broad shoulders and slim hips. Her reflection in the window, on the other hand, reminded her that her hair was twisted up in a sloppy topknot held in place by a pencil, and she wasn't wearing any makeup. How was she to know she'd have an unexpected visitor?

She cleared her throat. "What brings you out in this storm?"

"Oh, um, Mr. Bartholomew and I came to visit Cardinal Hollow."

"Is your friend from around here?"

"No. Thaddeus Bartholomew is my employer, actually. We heard Cardinal Hollow is a charming town."

When Evan mentioned the most famous wizard in Ceresland, Minna was unnerved. What she wouldn't give to meet the kingdom's former Head Wizard, much less work for him! Nevertheless, she pretended she'd never heard the man's name before, since most non-magical people would have no interest in such things.

She cleared her throat. "You picked a bad day for sightseeing."

"As it turns out."

The wizard's blue eyes twinkled in her direction and her cheeks grew warm again.

"Er...excuse me while I pour the hot chocolate."

She busied herself at the stove, wondering why her usual poise was deserting her. Ordinarily, she would be perfectly at ease, but the thunder must have jangled her nerves. Once she'd ladled the hot beverage into two mugs, she put a few slices of moist pound cake on a plate and arranged everything on a tray.

"It's ready." She glanced over her shoulder. "Would you like to sit in here or the fireplace?"

"Shh." Evan grinned and cocked his thumb toward the cocker spaniel, who had made himself comfortable on the blanket and fallen asleep. The sight of the vulnerable creature made her go all squishy inside.

"He's so sweet, but he has no collar or tag." Minna frowned. "I don't know if I'll be able to find his owner."

"Perhaps he's already with his new owner." Evan shrugged and reached for the tray. "You two seem made for one another."

Minna followed the young wizard into the living room. When she noticed the blazing glow lighting the empty fireplace and felt its heat, she gasped with delight.

"A logless fire spell! The only time I've ever seen one done successfully was at the Aldesbury Hotel. Most logless fire spells have the warmth of a snowball."

"I'm glad you like it. The secret is to use a slowly collapsing containment field, by the way. This particular fire will last about three hours."

"But how do you—" She broke off. "Oh, never mind. I don't know much about magic and probably wouldn't understand."

Minna sank down into a worn armchair, leaving the sofa to Evan. As the wizard sat facing the fire, the puppy ambled from the kitchen, stood on his hind legs, and stretched his paws toward the man's knees.

"The little beast woke up after all." She smiled. "I think he likes you."

"He's a charmer."

Once Evan lifted the dog into his lap, the tiny creature yawned and curled himself into a ball. The movement of the wizard's hands as he stroked the pup's fur drew her attention to the distinctive class ring he wore.

"You studied at the Aldesbury Magic Academy?"

"Yes, I graduated this past May." A note of pride registered in his voice.

"It's the best magic school in the country, I've heard."

"I'm quite grateful to have matriculated there. Where did you go school?"

"Cardinal Hollow Secondary." She forced a smile. "It offers magical theory as an elective."

Evan gave her a quizzical glance as he reached for his mug. "What a shame. I daresay many people possess untapped magical potential if they were only allowed to discover it."

"Perhaps, but you know how it is." She shrugged. "Some folks are leery of magic."

He blew gently across the surface of his hot cocoa. "One might as well be afraid of air or water."

"Exactly. People are frightened of things they can't understand."

"Yes." His gaze focused on the oil painting hung over the rough-hewn wooden mantle. The canvas depicted a dashing, exceptionally handsome man dressed in racing silks, posed in front of a thoroughbred dragon. "That's Wynn Westerfield with Crucible, isn't it?"

"Indeed, it is. Wynn Westerfield is my father."

His brows shot upward. "You're joking."

She laughed at his shocked expression. "Not in the least. I painted it from a rather famous photograph taken before the accident."

His lips parted as he stared at the canvas. "That's your work? You're a very talented artist."

"Thank you. I'm going to be teaching art to the youngest children at the local primary school this fall. Finger painting, mostly."

"Seems a waste of your abilities, if you don't mind me saying so."

"I'd like to do something else, but it's still too soon to leave Papa alone. Mama passed away last year and he's been rather lost without her."

To cover a sudden surge of grief, Minna took a piece of cake and nibbled the edges.

Evan's dismay seemed sincere. "I'm sorry for your loss."

"Thank you. She was quite a wonderful woman."

"I'm sure she was." He paused. "Where is your father right now?"

"Actually, he's at a dragon convention on the coast, making a speech and signing autographs."

"My mother won't believe me when I tell her we've met. She has a scrapbook of your father's photos and press clippings stashed somewhere."

"My mother always said Wynn Westerfield was a ladies' man before they met. To me, he's just Papa."

He peered into her face. "You resemble him a great deal."

"So I've been told."

To her dismay, a morsel of cake broke off and slipped down her shirt. Fortunately, his attention was focused on his hot chocolate and she managed to catch the cake as it fell into her lap.

"I'm sorry I won't have the chance to meet the great Wynn Westerfield." He sipped his chocolate and licked the froth from his lips. "Have you flown dragons, too?"

"Not for years. I used to exercise them around the paddock when we owned the ranch. Not the full-grown ones, of course. Just the younger dragons my father was grooming to race."

"That's exciting. I wanted to be a dragon jockey when I was a kid, but my ability with magic led me elsewhere."

The puppy turned on his back and snuggled into the wizard. As the conversation turned to the upcoming racing season, Minna was pleasantly surprised at Evan's extensive knowledge of the sport.

"So who do you think will win the Dragon National this year?" he asked finally.

"The odds makers favor Kent Magano, but Papa thinks Sam Brittany has the makings of a champion. He has the touch."

"It's not just about the jockeys, is it? Surely the dragons themselves play a role."

"Yes, of course, but without the right jockey, even the most magnificent dragon can't win."

"I suppose not." As Evan stroked the puppy's fur, the creature gave a great sigh of happiness. "The wizard who caused your father's racing accident just escaped from prison, didn't he?"

"Yes, he disappeared about ten days ago." Minna kept her tone light even though her emotions ran as hot as the logless fire spell. "Ned Rooney was a gambling addict who tried to fix the Dragon National Championship. He nearly killed my father and Crucible had to be destroyed."

"I was watching the race on a vidscreen when the crash happened." He shook his head. "Then, after the police arrested Rooney, I followed his trial.

Her laugh was mirthless. "So did I."

Evan drained the last of his hot chocolate and set the mug down on the coffee table nearby. "If you don't mind my asking, can your father use his arm at all?"

"A very little, but he can't race anymore. It's a good thing he isn't here to meet you, actually. He never liked magic or wizards before the crash, and he despises them completely now."

"I'd never want to be on the wrong side of Wynn Westerfield, so I'm very sorry to hear that." He glanced at the window. "Looks like the rain might be slowing. I should be able to leave soon."

"Are you at the Cardinal Hollow Inn?"

"As a matter of fact, I am. How did you know?"

"Unless you have friends in town, it's the only place to stay.

One of my former classmates works there." She put the empty mugs back onto the tray. "Excuse me a moment."

Minna took the tray into the kitchen, rinsed the mugs, and wiped away a few muddy paw prints from the tile floor. To her dismay, the dog had also left a puddle next to the blanket. After a quick glance to make sure she'd be unobserved, Minna evaporated the puddle with magic. Should she decide to keep the beast, she'd have to install a pet door.

By the time she returned to the living room, Evan had nodded off with the cocker spaniel nestled in the crook of his arm. The light from the magical fire bathed the scene in a beautiful golden glow. Charmed, Minna perched on the raised hearth and drank in the wizard's features. Boyishly handsome, with strong eyebrows that framed mischievous eyes, his nose was straight and even, and his cheekbones were high. Further, his clothes were made of the finest materials and tailored to fit his athletic frame. His shoes were new, too, and fashioned of dragon leather. In addition, the cashmere overcoat he'd left hanging in the kitchen had probably cost a small fortune.

Although she realized envy was beneath her, she couldn't suppress a wistful yearning for a small fraction of Evan's privileges. What must it be like to have enough money to dress like a fashion model and attend the finest school in the kingdom? Before her father's accident, she could have answered that question for herself. Now, the prosperity and carefree existence she'd enjoyed as a child seemed like ancient history. She gave the last remaining gold charm on her bracelet a wistful tap. As the dragon swung back and forth, she sighed. The other charms had been sold to pay for her mother's medical expenses in the last year of her life, and the custom replica of Crucible was the only one remaining.

When Evan began to snore softly, she stifled a giggle. He looked so innocent reclining on the sofa, with his full lips parted. The puppy stretched out a tiny paw to touch the man's chin, and Minna's heart melted for the second time that afternoon. She tiptoed into her room to retrieve a sketchpad, and spent the next few minutes capturing the scene on paper. Unfortunately, lightning struck near the house, and the accompanying thunder woke man and beast alike. As the puppy streaked under the sofa, Minna dropped her sketchbook and hastened over to the window to investigate a crash in the side yard.

"W-What's going on?" Evan sounded woozy.

"Lightning hit a tree, I think." A large branch lay on the ground, and the oak from which it had fallen was scorched and smoking. Minna surreptitiously used a swift bit of magic to make sure the damage was contained. "It's all right now."

"I guess I fell asleep." He paused. "What's this?"

She turned to discover the wizard had her sketchbook in his hands and was peering at her drawing. Her cheeks suddenly felt extraordinarily warm.

"Oh…I, um, just thought you and the puppy looked sweet together."

He shot her a dark glance. "You should have asked my permission before drawing my portrait."

"I didn't want to wake you." Humiliated beyond measure, Minna hastened to take the sketchbook from him. "Honestly, there's no reason to be so sensitive. I didn't mean any harm."

His chin lifted. "I don't much like being stared at when I'm dozing, thank you very much!"

Her temper flared. "Really? I had the impression you enjoy being stared at all the time."

A muscle in his jaw quivered. "That's my cue to go. If you'll excuse me, I'll get my coat."

As he strode into the kitchen, Minna felt a pang of genuine

remorse. Just because he'd caught her admiring him was no reason for her to be so churlish.

Evan returned, wearing his coat. "Thank you for the hot chocolate, Miss Westerfield. I'll see myself out."

"Wait." She tore the sketch from the sketchbook, folded it into a square, and pressed it into his hands. "I'm sorry for being rude just now...and for disturbing your privacy."

His expression softened. "I probably overreacted."

"You didn't. No hard feelings, I hope."

"Of course not." He gave her a crooked grin. "I was embarrassed to be caught sleeping, if you want to know the truth. What with all the thunder, I didn't sleep well last night." He tucked the folded paper into his coat pocket. "Listen, it's none of my business, but with magical abilities like yours, it's a shame you don't use them openly."

She feigned puzzlement. "I don't know what you're talking about."

"You don't have to pretend."

Any remorse she'd felt at her incivility shriveled up. "You're right. It's none of your business."

Without warning, the wizard slid his arm around her waist and pulled her close. The hair on her forearms and the back of her neck rose. Unbidden, her gaze was drawn to his full lips.

"W-What are you doing?"

He looked at her askance. "Come on, Miss Westerfield. Can't you feel the electricity between us?"

"I don't know what you mean." Shaken, she took a step back.

"We both have goose bumps." He pointed at her bare forearms. "A wizard can sense magic, especially when it's as powerful as yours."

"You've overstepped the mark, Mr. Valentine."

"I don't think I have." He raised one of his eyebrows. "Furthermore, I bet I'm not the only one who enjoys being stared at."

She gave him a level glance. "You're rather conceited, Mr. Valentine. Don't get struck by lightning on your way out."

Evan chuckled. "Oh, I was struck by lightning years ago, when we first met."

"But we've never met."

A flicker of disappointment crossed his features. "I didn't think you'd remember."

He left. After the door shut behind him, Minna peeked through the curtains at the window. Although it was still pouring, raindrops bounced away from the man as he sauntered down the sidewalk toward the gate. The wizard was bone dry in the midst of a downpour, even without an umbrella. If he had the ability to dodge the storm, why had he arrived at her house, soaking wet?

The cocker spaniel barked, staring up at her with winsome eyes.

"You're so cute, I'm going to call you Beast."

With no proper dog food at hand, she went into the kitchen to search for something more substantial than milk to fill the little creature's belly. As she scrambled a couple of eggs, she pondered the strange afternoon. Why would Evan press her to admit she was a wizard and then pretend they'd already formed an acquaintance? Even if they'd only chatted briefly at one of her father's public appearances, she would have remembered such a fashionably clad and handsome man.

While the cocker spaniel ate scrambled eggs, Minna set out a layer of old newspapers next to the side door.

"It's indoor plumbing for you while it's raining, Beast." She glanced at the puppy, perplexed. "Why would a powerful wizard and his apprentice be sightseeing in a backwater country town like Cardinal Hollow?"

The puppy merely finished his eggs and began to lick the plate.

"And why would Evan Valentine show up at my house in the midst of a squall with a lost dog?" She sighed. "Something's definitely fishy."

Her gaze riveted on the kitchen table, where a small, folded paper dragon sat next to the napkin holder. How had her dragon come to be in the kitchen? As she peered at its bright red color, however, she realized the paper was new and had writing on it. After she unfolded the dragon, a message was revealed.

"Mr. Bartholomew and I usually dine at six. See you then. Evan."

As a long-ago memory of evaluation day surfaced, she gasped. "It can't be!"

CHAPTER 3

PIXIE DUST

In the deserted dining room at the Cardinal Hollow Inn, Evan and Thaddeus waited for their meal to arrive. Although the cozy space held several tables and the fireplace crackled with a real fire, the two wizards were the only diners. Thaddeus gestured to a decanter on a nearby sideboard and it flew into his hand. After he splashed a bit of port into his glass, he sent the cut-glass bottle floating back to its place.

"I can't believe you've ordered only a cup of soup for dinner. How do you expect to exist?"

"I don't seem to have any appetite this evening." Evan checked his watch for the umpteenth time. "I'm sorry, Mr. Bartholomew, but I don't think Miss Westerfield is coming."

"Are you sure you told her the right time?"

He gave his employer a rueful glance. "Yes, but she evidently decided not to accept my invitation."

"You failed to win her over with your considerable charm?" Thaddeus chuckled in a deep voice. "I never thought I'd see the day when Evan Valentine met his match."

"She's more than my match. In fact, the dragon jockey's

daughter has inherited his steely disposition." He sighed. "Maybe you should speak with her in the morning, alone."

"Why?"

"My recollection of her was obviously more flattering than her recollection of me." He frowned. "She didn't remember me at all."

"You look quite different than you did when you were twelve, so I'm not surprised." The elderly wizard reached over to pat his arm. "Buck up, lad. We'll find a way to sort things out tomorrow."

"I hope you're right." Relief swept over him when a beautiful girl appeared in the doorway of the dining room. "Here she is."

He and Thaddeus hastened to stand as Minna approached. The young woman was clad in a simple short black sheath and red high heels. Her nutmeg-colored hair floated in a waterfall around her shoulders, and the cut of the dress made the most of her figure.

"I'm sorry I'm late." She glanced between Evan and Thaddeus. "I really couldn't make up my mind whether or not I should come at all."

"I'm glad you did." Evan held her chair while she was seated. "Miss Westerfield, this is Mr. Bartholomew."

Thaddeus beamed. "I'm delighted to make your acquaintance."

"It's truly an honor to meet you, sir." Minna turned to Evan. "Why didn't you tell me who you were right off?"

"I wasn't sure you'd remember, and then it would have been terribly awkward. I wouldn't have blamed you, of course." He shrugged. "It's been several years, after all, and we met only briefly."

"You were admitted to the academy, obviously. I'm glad for

you." A ripple of sadness crossed her lovely features. "A great many things happened in my life since then."

A server entered the dining room with a tray of food and approached their table. "Oh, hello, Minna. May I bring you something?"

"Hello, Julianne. Tea and a small dinner salad with oil and vinegar, please."

"Right away."

Julianne set a small cup of chicken corn chowder in front of Evan. Thaddeus had ordered a more substantial meal of steak medallions, steamed broccoli, and mashed potatoes, and as the server put the plate on the table, Evan felt his mouth water.

"Er...would you bring me a baked potato loaded with bacon, cheese, and sour cream?"

"Right away, Mr. Valentine." Empty tray in hand, she hastened from the room.

Minna nodded toward the table. "Please don't wait on my account. I'm not terribly hungry this evening."

Thaddeus's beard twitched in a smile. "You and my apprentice seem to be suffering from the same affliction. For some reason, however, his appetite has improved."

Evan shot the older wizard a level glance, but Thaddeus blithely ignored him in favor of cutting into his steak.

Minna cocked her head. "May I ask why you've come to Cardinal Hollow, Mr. Bartholomew? I presume it wasn't to gift me with a puppy."

"Of course not." Evan picked up his spoon. "That was my idea."

Thaddeus cleared his throat. "What my apprentice means to say is he was trying to break the ice, as it were, before putting forth a proposal. You see, Miss Westerfield, Evan and I need your help."

"I can't imagine why the former Head Wizard of Ceresland

and his apprentice need my help with anything." She frowned. "Does this involve my father?"

"Not at all."

She sighed. "Now I'm terribly confused."

"A visual aid will be useful, I think." He conjured a filmy white barrier midair, like a fine linen curtain. "This represents the barrier separating one reality from another."

Evan winced. "Don't broach the topic gently, sir. Just leap right in with both feet."

Thaddeus shrugged. "There's no need to sugar-coat the facts with Miss Westerfield, lad. As you pointed out in such an admiring fashion, she has a steely disposition."

Minna glanced at Evan. "I've a steely disposition?"

"I meant it as a compliment."

He stirred his corn chowder with feigned unconcern, but inwardly he was dismayed. Thaddeus seemed perversely determined to embarrass him at every opportunity. Before Thaddeus could continue, Julianne brought Minna's salad and tea, along with Evan's baked potato.

"May I bring you anything else?"

Thaddeus winked. "We are perfect, my dear."

The young lady giggled. "I'll be back to check on you in a few minutes."

After she left, the elderly man gestured toward the transparent curtain once more.

"As I was saying, this represents the barrier that separates one reality from another."

"You're talking about parallel dimensions?" Even as Minna stabbed her salad, she made a sound of disbelief. "That concept has never been proven."

"I've proven it, I can assure you." Using his fork, Thaddeus made a downward, jagged motion in the milky whiteness, forming a large hole. "Unfortunately, a certain wizard has managed to break through this barrier and in doing so, created a tear, like so. The unsealed rift has disrupted the magical balance in our universe."

"I find this difficult to believe."

"Difficult, yes, but not impossible." Evan leaned forward. "Haven't you noticed the kingdom has been having more frequent and violent lightning storms? This strange weather is caused by the rift."

She shook her head. "Forgive me, but I'd have to see this rift for myself."

"I'm glad to hear that." Thaddeus made the torn curtain disappear with a wave of his fingers. "As it so happens, solving this problem requires the efforts of three extremely powerful and well-trained wizards. That's where you come in, Miss Westerfield."

"Other than you two, I'm not acquainted with any wizards like that." Minna lifted a forkful of salad to her lips.

Evan nearly choked on a mouthful of soup. "You must be joking!"

Thaddeus lifted a quelling hand. "Easy, lad. On some topics, a gentle approach is indeed best."

Evan put down his spoon. "All right, Miss Westerfield, let's review some history. After your father's accident, an anonymous donor set up a full scholarship for you at Aldesbury Magic Academy. Even though you were one of the most talented youngsters the school had ever tested, your father refused to let you attend. Thereafter, you've secretly been studying magic on your own."

She gasped. "How could you possibly know that?"

"I told him." Thaddeus fixed his brown eyes on Minna over the rims of his glasses. "Once your father refused his permission for you to matriculate at the Academy, your dear mother quietly contacted me to ask about booklists for homeschooled wizards."

"My mother contacted the Head Wizard of Ceresland about me?" Minna peered at him. "I'd no idea."

"Nancy believed your father was in no state of mind to forbid you from developing your abilities. Ordinarily, I would have refused to interfere, but I dislike talent going to waste. After some deliberation, I agreed to oversee your education. I kept in constant contact with her regarding your progress and even came to visit you twice a year."

"I don't mean to be difficult, but I don't recall having been introduced to you before today."

"Oh, I wasn't myself. No, I was Mr. Bodkins, the short fat jolly fellow from the fictitious Homeschooled Students for Sorcery Board of Education."

Her jaw dropped. "That was you?"

His eyes twinkled as he smoothed down his beard. "In disguise. As you see, I'm far more handsome than Mr. Bodkins."

Evan swallowed a bite of potato. "Now that your training isn't a secret any longer, Miss Westerfield, will you join us?"

"Legally, I can't. I haven't taken my wizard exam yet, and if the authorities catch me practicing wizardry without a proper license, I could be barred from the practice of magic altogether."

"Your work is permitted as long as it's under my direct supervision." Thaddeus nodded at Evan. "If it sets your mind at ease, my apprentice doesn't have his license either. He won't be sitting for the exam until it's offered this fall."

"I've registered for that particular exam as well." She bit her lower lip. "I just have to find the right moment to break it to my father."

Evan blinked. "You're over eighteen, Minna. Your father has to let you go sometime."

"You make it sound simple, but you don't know him like I do." She sighed. "I-I have a few days before he gets back from his business trip. Could we get the rift sealed before then?"

"Possibly so, but it won't be easy." Thaddeus counted off the challenges on his fingers. "We must first travel to the parallel dimension, locate the wizard responsible for creating the rift, and then bring him back to face justice. He used a purloined magical letter opener to breach the barrier, and we can't fail to retrieve it."

"And we have to do all that without a fuss," Evan said. "You see, the letter opener is Mr. Bartholomew's."

Her eyebrows rose. "Oh?"

"The thief broke into my house and stole it." Thaddeus scowled. "If anyone else discovers such an object exists, chaos would be unleashed."

The corners of her lips quirked up in a smile. "I suppose having unlicensed wizards on the case would help keep the matter under wraps."

"Yes, but there's also the question of motivation." Thaddeus's gaze slid toward his apprentice. "My apprentice believes you're perfect for the task."

She gave Evan a quizzical glance. "I can't imagine why."

Evan cleared his throat. "The thief is Ned Rooney. I thought perhaps you might enjoy the task of catching him."

Her smile faded and she grew pale. "I see."

As Minna struggled to maintain her composure, guilt washed over Evan. "Please forgive me if I misjudged the situation. I didn't mean to reopen old wounds."

When she met his gaze, her eyes were burning with surprising intensity.

"There's no need to apologize, Mr. Valentine. In fact, I'm

eager to help." She folded her napkin by the side of her plate. "Mr. Bartholomew, you may pick me up after breakfast tomorrow morning. I hope my puppy may accompany us? I can't leave him in the house alone."

"He's more than welcome," Thaddeus said.

"If you'll excuse me, I need to purchase dog food before the pet store closes for the evening. Please don't get up."

Minna left the dining room without a backward glance.

Thaddeus picked up his fork. "That went better than I'd expected."

"She seems upset." Evan sighed. "I hope we're doing the right thing, sir."

"Miss Westerfield is in dire need of closure, and we need her help." The older wizard gave him an emphatic nod. "We're doing the right thing, lad. Never doubt it."

MINNA CARRIED a bag of puppy chow, a collar, and a leash for Beast to the sales counter at the pet store. The store's proprietor smiled as he bagged her purchases.

"I didn't know you had a dog, Minna."

"I do now. He's a stray, but terribly sweet."

"We had a litter of the cutest cocker spaniel puppies, but I sold the last one today."

Somehow the news didn't surprise her. "Really? Who bought him?"

The man shook his head. "He was a young, nice-looking chap, but I've not seen him around here before." He put change in her hand. "Odd weather we've been having lately, wouldn't you say?"

"Yes, it's quite out of the ordinary."

Evan was leaning up against a lamppost nearby when she

emerged from the shop. He straightened and reached for her shopping bag.

"May I walk you home?"

"Thank you."

The night temperatures were pleasant as they strolled down the street, but spectacular lightning storms lit the horizon as if a war were being waged in the sky.

She slid Evan a reproachful glance. "You really didn't need to buy me a dog, you know."

He shrugged. "My uncle used to say women liked dogs, so I thought I'd take a chance. Besides which, I owe you a debt of gratitude."

"I can't imagine how."

"When you decided not to enroll at the Academy, the person who donated your scholarship allowed the school to give it to me. Since I never would have been able to attend otherwise, a puppy doesn't even begin to balance the scale."

Astonishment brought a smile to her face. "I'm glad you told me. I always wondered if you'd enrolled."

"Because of you, my life changed completely."

"Your gratitude should be reserved for the generous donor, not me."

"I'm grateful to you both, actually, but since the donor remains anonymous, I can only express my feelings to you."

For the next few moments, only the sound of distant thunder and the soft click of her high heels on the pavement broke the silence. As she and Evan neared the white picket fence that surrounded her house, he cleared his throat.

"The past few years must have been very difficult for you. I admire the way you've pursued your magical education against all odds."

"My mother always looked out for me." Minna swallowed hard. "I miss her very much."

To her dismay, her voice rasped at the end. Worse, grief suddenly gripped her by the throat and squeezed it shut. The more she fought back tears, however, the less she could control them. Moisture began to stream from her eyes, and she brushed it away with her fingertips.

"Sorry." She shook her head. "I don't know why my emotions seem to be so volatile lately."

Evan produced a handkerchief. "Take this."

"Thank you."

He ushered her inside the gate and carried her shopping bag to the porch. "Are you going to be all right?"

"I'll be fine."

"Look." He gestured toward the small yard, where luminescent winged beetles were glowing intermittently. "Fireflies are out tonight."

"So they are. My mother used to call them fairies and I believed her."

"There are worse things to believe." He paused. "See you tomorrow."

"See you tomorrow."

Evan retraced his steps down the short path toward the street, disappearing into the darkness beyond the gate. Minna picked up the shopping bag and entered her house, where Beast was wriggling with delight at her return. Smiling through her tears, she buckled the new collar around his neck and let him out to roam the yard while she sat on the porch steps to keep watch.

Ned Rooney.

Just thinking the name roiled her stomach. She'd only attended one day of his trial, and that was the day he was sentenced...

The wizard was nervous as he glanced over his shoulder at the courtroom full of reporters and other interested parties. Wynn had stayed away, but Minna and her mother were there, along with Aunt Bettina.

Rooney took the stand to read a statement of apology just before his sentence was handed down, but his insincerity grated Minna's nerves and made her angrier than she thought possible. She knew very little magic at that point, but when the disgraced wizard climbed down from the stand, she caused him to trip and sprawl flat on his face. After the bailiff hauled him to his feet, blood streaming from his nose, Rooney had stared right at her. She stared back, unblinking. Everyone else assumed the fall was an accident but he knew better—and the fear showed in his eyes. She'd never been so glad in her life to make a powerful wizard afraid.

Aunt Bettina snickered. "Too bad Rooney didn't break his neck."

"Ned Rooney is a man to be pitied," Minna's mother said. "We must find it in our hearts to forgive him, or our hatred will infect our souls."

Aunt Bettina rolled her eyes. "You've always been a far better person than I am, Nancy."

Mama always was a better person than I am, too. I can't forgive Ned Rooney—not ever. If he really was guilty of opening a magical rift, the transgression would be one of many iniquities he'd committed. Not only had her father never been the same physically, but the family's reduced financial circumstances and stress had contributed to her mother's decline. As Minna thought about what her life could have been, renewed anger spread through her veins like poison.

She brought Beast into the house and poured him a bowl of kibble. As the puppy attacked the food, Minna went off to locate a small suitcase. If Ned Rooney suspected how much her hatred of him had grown over the years, he'd flee into so many parallel dimensions, nobody would ever find him. Further-more, if Evan and Thaddeus had known how badly she yearned to mete out revenge, they would never have asked for her help. It was a good thing she didn't intend to tell them.

While she packed clothes for her upcoming journey, a flash of illumination presaged the return of another lightning storm. Although unaccompanied by rain this time, thunderstorms continued to roll through Cardinal Hollow until well past midnight. Beast curled up on the counterpane next to her, his warm body providing a comforting presence.

By morning, sunshine poured in through the windows, and Minna's tears had turned into cool determination. Not altogether certain what to wear for the journey, she donned a lilac blouse, tucked it into her best pair of jeans, and twisted her long hair into a loose braid. Once she was dressed, she brought Beast into the kitchen to fill his bowl with chow. The dog's floppy ears completely covered the dish as he ate, and his jeweled, light blue leather collar sparkled in the sunlight.

Over freshly brewed coffee and toast, she felt almost as if her own tail were wagging. She'd managed to push her anger at Ned Rooney to one side for the moment in favor of an overwhelming sense of relief. Her secret life as a student of magic had weighed upon her more heavily than she'd admitted until now. Once she left Cardinal Hollow, she'd be free to be herself —for a few days at least. Not only that, but she would also have the opportunity to work with Thaddeus Bartholomew, the most renowned wizard of the age.

Minna deposited her suitcase by the front door and went about fashioning a travel box for Beast. As she was rummaging in the pantry for a suitably shaped cardboard container, however, she heard heavy footsteps crossing the porch.

"Argh! Why did they have to come early?" She made a

sound of aggravation. "Well, they'll just have to wait until Beast and I are ready to go."

As she left the pantry, the front door opened, and her father's booming voice rang out.

"Good morning! I smell coffee!"

She gasped. "Oh, pixie dust!"

Minna froze in a panic, but there was nothing she could do. Moments later, Wynn Westerfield joined her in the kitchen, ducking to clear the doorframe. At six feet and four inches, stooping through doorways had become a habit for the ex-dragon jockey. Because he was still shockingly handsome despite his scarred arm, women usually dissolved into inanity in his presence. Minna never thought she'd be one of them.

"You're home early, Papa. Um...I, uh...good morning." She gulped. "I'll pour you some coffee."

"Thanks." Using his good arm, Wynn slid his duffle bag off his shoulder and lowered it to the floor while Beast scampered at his feet. "Is this your puppy?"

"Ah, well, you know...you're gone so much these days, I thought he would keep me company."

"Good idea."

She poured her father a mug of freshly brewed coffee, trying to quell the trembling of her hands. How on earth was she to explain it when Thaddeus Bartholomew and Evan came to pick her up in a few minutes?

Minna brought him the coffee. "I didn't expect you home for days yet."

"Neither did I." He chuckled. "The convention hall lost power after my speech last night, and the roof began to leak from the rain. Everyone was leaving anyway, so the promoters canceled the remaining events."

Her eyebrows rose. "What about your fee?"

"Don't worry, the promoters were more than fair. I wanted

to save myself the cost of a hotel room, so I drove all night through a spectacular lightning storm. I probably should have called, but I didn't want to wake you."

"There was lightning here, too." She gestured toward the cocker spaniel. "This is Beast."

Her father chuckled as he put his mug on the table and knelt to pet the wiggling bundle of fur. "You named him Beast?"

"It seemed appropriate. Want some toast with your coffee?"

"I got breakfast on the road, thanks."

When a woodpecker banged on the side of the house, Minna visibly flinched.

Wynn peered at her. "Why are you so nervous?"

"Uh, I'm waiting for some friends to pick me up."

"This early in the morning?" He took in her appearance. "You look very nice. Does one of your visitors happen to be a boyfriend?"

"No. They're colleagues rather than friends, actually."

He peered at her, clearly puzzled. "Teachers from the primary school?"

"No." She cleared her throat. "Actually, I've been offered a job. More of a temporary internship, really, and it involves—"

A knock on the front door interrupted her revelation.

"That's my ride." Minna took a deep breath. "Come on and I'll introduce you."

CHAPTER 4

HARLEQUIN HALL

ynn followed Minna with Beast nestled in the crook of his arm. When she opened the front door, Thaddeus Bartholomew stood on the other side, hat in hand. Evan was leaning against the porch post in dapper attire, his arms folded across his chest. When he noticed the imposing figure just behind Minna, he straightened.

"Wynn Westerfield!" A delighted grin spread across his features. "It's an honor to meet you, sir."

She braced herself. "Papa, this is Mr. Bartholomew and Mr. Valentine. Gentlemen, my father returned home unexpectedly just this morning, and I haven't had the opportunity to tell him the news about our venture."

The older wizard beamed. "Call me Thaddeus, Mr. Westerfield. I'm retired now, but I was formerly the Head Wizard of Ceresland."

To Minna's dismay, her father ignored Thaddeus's outstretched hand.

"I know exactly who you are." Wynn leveled an icy glance at Evan. "Are you a wizard, too?"

The young man lifted his chin. "Yes, sir. I'm a recent graduate of the Aldesbury Magic Academy. I was Valedictorian."

"Evan is my apprentice, Mr. Westerfield." Thaddeus nodded toward Minna. "We've solicited your daughter's assistance in a matter of great importance."

"We want nothing to do with wizards here." Wynn stepped back and reached for the door. "Good day to you both."

"Stop!" Minna's voice rang out. "Mama is the one who introduced me to Mr. Bartholomew, Papa. He's a long-time acquaintance of mine."

"That's impossible. I would have known."

"Mama didn't tell you everything, and neither have I." She swallowed hard. "Mr. Bartholomew has been supervising my magical education."

Her father's face, already tired and drawn from lack of sleep, took on a wounded expression.

"You've been studying magic after I expressly forbade it?"

"You forbade me from attending the Academy, Papa, and therefore I didn't go. But Mama encouraged me to develop my talent in my spare time." Although her father's eyes narrowed, her spine straightened. "Mr. Bartholomew and I are to work together on a project. I'll be back in..." She cast a quizzical glance at Thaddeus.

"Three days should do it, allowing for travel time."

Wynn bristled. "You're not going anywhere without my permission!"

"I'm eighteen years old and you have to let me go sometime." She hated using Evan's words, but they seemed appropriate. "Trust me, Papa. I know what I'm doing."

He scowled. "You're not in possession of all the facts."

"I wish I could have told you in some other way." She was

shaking as she picked up her overnight bag. "Please look after Beast while I'm gone. His leash is hanging on a hook in the kitchen. When I return, I'll introduce you to someone else you haven't met—your daughter, the wizard Minna Westerfield."

While Thaddeus stayed behind to speak with Wynn, Evan reached for her bag and ushered her down the path.

"I'm sorry, Minna." His voice was low. "Standing up to your father must have been difficult."

"Yes." Her throat and eyes burned with emotion, but she managed a brief smile. "It's the first time I've ever gone against his wishes on anything. I hope it gets easier."

When she reached the street, she was surprised to see a black limousine parked behind her father's car. Evan opened the rear passenger door and beckoned her over.

"In you go."

She slid inside, enjoying the feel of the leather seats and luxurious details. Evan stowed her bag in the trunk and then slid behind the wheel. As they waited for Thaddeus to join them, she caught Evan's gaze in the rear-view mirror.

"I haven't been in one of these in years. Do you and Mr. Bartholomew always travel in such style?"

Evan shrugged. "It's a lot faster than riding the train and a great deal more fun."

"Oh, before I forget..." She returned his handkerchief to him. "I used a cleaning spell on it."

"Hang on, I have something to show you." His smile was mischievous as he did something to the linen square, out of sight.

She craned her neck. "What are you doing?"

"You'll see. Put out your hand." He folded the fabric into the shape of a white rosebud. When he put it on her outstretched palm, the flower bloomed. "That's for you. Keep it...for luck."

The kind gesture brought a smile to her lips. "You're sitting too far away for me to kiss you this time."

She felt the blood rush to her face as she realized what she'd said. She and Evan weren't twelve years old any longer, and kisses took on a whole other significance than before. Apparently, he appreciated that full well because his ears turned pink and he cleared his throat.

"I'll take a raincheck, then."

Completely embarrassed, she focused her attention on Thaddeus and her father instead. She couldn't hear what they were saying to one another, but the wizard's body language seemed almost apologetic. In turn, Wynn was stiff, unyielding, and bristling with resentment.

"If Mr. Bartholomew is trying to persuade Papa, he's wasting his breath. My father is a man of firm opinions."

"Oh, I don't know. The old boy can be very persuasive." Evan shrugged. "Perhaps he's giving your father something to think about while you're gone."

"Maybe so, but I apologize for Papa's rudeness, nevertheless. It's not as if you and Mr. Bartholomew have ever done anything to him personally."

"From your father's perspective, we're taking his daughter away. Perhaps if the situation were reversed, I'd be rude as well."

Moments later, Thaddeus came ambling down the path, seemingly unscathed. Once he climbed into the front passenger seat, he smiled and rubbed his hands together, as if in anticipation.

"Shall we?"

"Is everything all right?" she asked.

"Don't worry. Your father and I have come to an uneasy understanding for the time being." The elderly wizard gave her a reassuring nod. "I'll try to smooth things a little more over when we return."

Wynn and Beast were watching from the yard as the long black car pulled away from the curb. Minna held up a hand in farewell, and then resolutely faced forward.

"Where are we heading, gentlemen?"

"My home, Harlequin Hall," said Thaddeus. "Just outside Aldesbury City."

As they left Cardinal Hollow behind, Minna was grateful neither Thaddeus nor Evan felt the need to make idle chitchat. Because of the abrupt way she and her father had parted, she was content to be left alone with her thoughts for a while. She would have preferred to break the news of her magical training more gently, but she supposed her father would have reacted badly whichever way she put it. In addition, although she felt a pang at being separated from Beast, it was just as well he'd stayed home. The winsome puppy would surely take her father's mind off her rebellion.

After an hour of driving past farms, orchards and the occasional dragon ranch, Thaddeus finally broke the silence.

"It pains me to say so, but Ned Rooney is quite a talented wizard."

Evan shot Thaddeus a sharp glance. "Why would you say that? The man's a scoundrel of the worst sort!"

"Yes, but he's a scoundrel who managed to break into my home and steal my letter opener. Furthermore, he opened the rift in such a clever spot, it almost escaped my notice."

Minna leaned forward, intrigued. "Where was that?"

"The large infinity mirror in the entranceway, where the edges of the rift blend in with the reflection." He shook his head. "The housekeeper found it by accident."

"That's a funny story." Evan grinned. "The poor woman

was dusting the mirror and nearly fell through. Her screaming woke me from a sound sleep."

"I liked Mrs. Purell's work, so it's not that funny, really." Thaddeus frowned. "The woman gave notice right then and there, and left the household in the lurch."

Evan scoffed. "She knew she was working for a wizard. Where was her sense of humor?"

Minna suppressed a smile. "Mr. Bartholomew, it was very kind of you to correspond with my mother about me. She had few people to turn to for advice."

"Why is that?" Evan asked.

"Mama said her society family disapproved of her marriage to a dragon rider so much they cut her out of their lives. Nancy Minerva Masters was supposed to marry a man with a title or a gentleman of great means."

Evan snorted. "What snobs! Wynn Westerfield has more talent in his thumb than a boatload of lords, earls, or moneyed elites."

Thaddeus gave his apprentice a reproving glance. "Snobbish relatives are still relatives and perhaps ought not be insulted quite so freely."

"I suppose not." Evan caught Minna's eye in the rear-view mirror. "No offense meant."

"None taken. I've never actually met most of my maternal relatives, so insults about them don't bother me in the least." Minna shrugged. "In fact, the only relative I know is Great-Aunt Bettina. She's not a snob."

"If your relatives realized what a lovely girl you are, I guarantee they would be thoroughly ashamed of themselves for shunning you for the last eighteen years," Thaddeus said.

"That's very sweet of you, Mr. Bartholomew."

"Wait a minute." Evan's scowl was exaggerated. "To *her*

you pay flowery compliments, yet I must grovel for the most meager approval?"

"Such is the life of a lowly apprentice, lad. You're fortunate I don't make you scrub floors."

"I daresay I'd likely do an abysmal job."

"I *am* looking for a new housekeeper."

"Keep looking, sir."

The good-humored interplay between the two wizards lifted Minna's mood. Soon thereafter, the trio stopped for lunch at a farmhouse that had been converted into a restaurant. Once they resumed their journey, Thaddeus insisted on taking the wheel. Although Minna offered to drive the rest of the way, the elderly wizard shook his head.

"We'll be hitting traffic soon, but I know a shortcut."

As Thaddeus had predicted, once they neared the city, red brake lights were visible as far as the eye could see and their pace slowed.

Evan cleared his throat. "What about that shortcut?"

The elderly wizard nodded. "Indeed, it's time to turn off the beaten path, wouldn't you say?"

"Tally-ho." Evan glanced back at Minna. "Hang on, Miss Westerfield."

Without further conversation, the limo's wheels left the road and the car lurched vertically, as if it were an elevator.

Minna gasped in shock. "What's going on?"

"We're flying, of course." Evan gave her a delighted smile. "Didn't I tell you riding in the limo was more fun than taking the train?"

"Why didn't you warn me?" Minna's stomach dropped as they gained height and she felt disoriented. "What if I had a tendency toward air sickness?"

"If you become nauseated, roll the window down and stick

your head out." Evan snickered. "Just try not to get sick on any passing birds."

She glared. "Thanks."

"Have you never been in a flying car before?" Thaddeus asked.

"No. I didn't even know such things existed."

"Think of it like riding a dragon," Thaddeus said. "I know you've done that."

"But dragons have wings!" she sputtered.

"If wings would make you feel more comfortable, so be it."

A pair of leathery wings sprouted from the automobile's sideboards and began to flap up and down in a leisurely fashion.

Evan groaned and rolled his eyes. "Now you're just showing off, sir."

Thaddeus vibrated with laughter. "You must allow an old wizard a few pleasures."

Once the limo reached cruising altitude, Minna managed to relax enough to enjoy the view of the city below. When Thaddeus passed over a semi-circular stadium from which a series of deep canyons emanated, a thrill of excitement shot through her.

"Oh, there's Aldesbury Dragon Park! The course runs a total of thirty miles, and it took a team of fourteen wizard engineers over six months to build. The vidscreens in the stadium are wider than four dragons and taller than two trolls."

"Yes, the park is an amazing feat of construction." Thaddeus nodded. "The Bartholomew family has owned a season box since it opened."

"Have you really? My envy is showing, I'm afraid." Evan chuckled. "I've never seen a dragon race in person, but my uncle and I used to watch them on the vidscreen at the pub around the corner."

"I've not been to the races since the accident." Minna sighed. "Even if we could afford it, Papa can't bring himself to enter the stadium."

Not too long thereafter, a large mountaintop estate drew her eye. The exterior of the alabaster structure was whimsical and rambling, with crenelated walls, gracefully peaked towers, and verdant, manicured gardens. As the limo drew closer, an artificial waterfall became visible.

"Who lives in that magnificent castle, do you know?"

"Let's find out, shall we?" Thaddeus turned the wheel toward the estate and the limo began to descend.

Minna's eyebrows drew together. "You don't have to make a detour on my account."

Evan gave her a sidelong glance. "Mr. Bartholomew is teasing you, Miss Westerfield. That's Harlequin Hall. The castle has been in his family for generations."

Her jaw dropped. "You don't live in that enormous place alone, do you, Mr. Bartholomew?"

"Not exactly. Evan took up residence shortly after graduation, and I employ a small staff as well. I confess, having a young person around has lifted my spirits considerably."

His apprentice laughed. "I'll remind you of that next time you're vexed with me."

Thaddeus set the car down on the long driveway leading to the castle. The wings disappeared, and as soon as the car came to a stop in the enormous motor court, Minna jumped out onto the decorative pavers.

"I hope you don't mind if I look at the view?"

Without waiting for an answer, she dashed toward a lookout nearby, built in the shape of a covered gazebo. Aldesbury City spread out in all its splendor below, and the kingdom of Ceresland beyond that. She took the opportunity to find familiar landmarks through the long lens of a spyglass mounted to the stone railing.

Evan joined her. "The view's inspiring, don't you think?"

"Incredible."

As she gazed through the spyglass, however, an electrical storm began to lash the city. Seconds later, rumbling thunder reached her ears. She recoiled and her mouth went dry.

"I've never seen lightning without clouds before."

"It's definitely not natural." He frowned as more bolts of lightning lit the sky. "It seems we landed just in time."

Thaddeus called out as he waited next to the limousine. "Come, children, let's go inside before we tempt fate. We've a universe to save, and we can't do our best if we've been burnt to a crisp."

Minna hastened to join the elderly wizard, but Evan circled around behind the limo to open the trunk.

"Go on ahead. I'll get the bags and meet you inside."

She took one last glance at the view. "Don't linger overlong. The storm is heading this way."

Thaddeus escorted her toward Harlequin Hall. They crossed over a quaint bowed bridge, where she paused to admire the stream passing underneath. A fanciful wolf sculpture set at the water's edge wagged its metallic tail and gave a long, low whistle.

She rolled her eyes. "Is the wolf your idea or is it historical in nature?"

"It's Evan's doing, actually. I let him try his hand at landscape design when he came to work for me."

"How terribly creative."

Over the sound of gurgling water, she heard a melodic humming. "Where is that music coming from?"

"Singing frogs, of course." He pointed to the banks of the stream. "They like to nestle in those mossy clumps just there."

She cocked her head to listen. "They're humming a tune in four-part harmony!"

"You should be flattered. Ordinarily, they greet me with a funeral march."

"The frogs are a nice touch. Are they your doing?"

"Indeed, they are. My childhood nickname was Tadpole, so frogs are a recurring theme at Harlequin Hall."

"My mother was always fond of frogs."

The castle doors magically opened inward as Minna and Thaddeus drew near. Inside, majestic, curved staircases on either side of the two-story entrance hall gave the space a grand feel, and the white marble tile under her feet shone like ice. A charming frog medallion had been artfully positioned in the center of the floor, but she barely spared the ornamental mosaic a glance due to the infinity mirror on the far wall. The six-foot-tall, glassy surface drew her in with its mesmerizing reflection.

Awestruck, she glanced at Thaddeus. "Is that the rift?"

"That's the one."

When she approached the mirror with an outstretched hand, her reflection did the same, dozens of times over. As her fingers passed through what should have been solid glass, she made a sound of disbelief.

"It feels like whipped cream."

His bushy eyebrows rose. "I hadn't thought of it that way, but I suppose it does."

Thaddeus stuck an index finger into the rift and made a stirring motion. Ripples spread outward, as if he'd dropped a pebble into a pond. He blew on it, and the surface bounced in response.

Evan entered the castle, laden with luggage. "Playing with the rift again, sir?"

The elderly wizard's neat, white beard split with mirth. "I

just can't leave well enough alone, can I? Please show Minna to my great-granddaughter's room, and I'll meet you both in the drawing room before dinner."

She blinked. "What about the rift?"

"We can't solve the problem on an empty stomach, can we? Let's plan our next move over a nice, hot meal."

As Thaddeus ambled off, humming the frogs' cheerful tune under his breath, Minna exchanged a glance with Evan.

"Now that I've seen the rift, I'm especially glad I didn't bring Beast. He probably would have darted into the mirror and I'd never see him again."

"That would have been dreadful." He shuddered and jerked his head toward one of the staircases. "Shall we?"

Once they'd ascended to the next floor, Evan sent his and Thaddeus's bags floating down the hall to the left.

"You're the other way, in the tower. I think you'll like your room."

He led her down the right-hand corridor until they reached the entrance to a circular staircase. A few moments later, they'd mounted the stairs and stepped through a doorway into a spacious, completely round bedchamber decorated in lilac— the same color as Minna's blouse. Enchanted, she rushed past Evan and spun around in delight.

"Oh, how beautiful! It's like something from a fairy tale!"

A white canopy bed graced the far curved wall, with a matching wardrobe nearby. Underneath the southeast-facing window, a drafting table awaited. Skylights set into the rotunda ceiling allowed additional illumination to saturate the room. A balcony afforded Minna an unobstructed view of Aldesbury City, albeit one marred with an unnatural lightning storm.

Evan lowered her bag onto the foot of the bed and joined her on the balcony. "Would you like a tour of the castle?"

"Oh, yes, I would." She glanced back at her bedroom. "Mr. Bartholomew said this was his great-granddaughter's room, but I didn't think he had any family."

"I honestly don't know. Although Mr. Bartholomew and I have a very cordial relationship, he's still my employer and I don't ask him personal questions. Perhaps you'll have better luck." He turned to leave. "I'll meet you downstairs in ten minutes for that tour. We don't have time to see much before dinner, but we'll fit in the library at least."

"That sounds perfect."

After he disappeared into the stairwell, Minna hastened to explore the adjacent bathroom. The frog motif was represented in the shower tile and as a decorative crest on the monogrammed towels. She unpacked her toiletries, brushed her hair, and freshened her makeup. As she reapplied her lipstick, she smiled at her reflection. Maybe she did enjoy being stared at—a little.

In the next moment, she took herself to task for the thought. Not only was Evan Valentine conceited, but he'd deceived her with Beast. Why should she care if the young wizard found her attractive? Besides which, she had secrets of her own regarding Ned Rooney, and didn't have any interest in playing the flirt. She reached for a tissue to wipe off the lipstick, but then she let her hand fall to her side. There was nothing wrong with putting her best foot forward.

Minna descended to the entrance hall, where Evan was lounging on the bottom step of the staircase. He'd donned a dinner jacket and combed his golden mane, and as he stood, the light from the chandelier reflected off his fair hair like a halo.

"I hope you found everything you needed?" he asked.

"Yes, thanks." Her gaze rested on his attire. "Perhaps I should have put on a dress for dinner?"

"I'm only wearing a jacket because Mr. Bartholomew insists. I think you look perfect the way you are." He flashed her a smile. "Let me show you the library before we join him in the drawing room. In my opinion, the library is the best part of the castle."

CHAPTER 5

TIMING IS EVERYTHING

Upon entering the two-story library, Minna couldn't help but gasp. The collection of leather-bound books was larger than any personal library she'd ever seen before. Sliding ladders gave access to the gallery above, huge oil paintings graced the walls, and freestanding sculptures here and there made the vast room look like a museum. Despite that, clusters of seating arrangements allowed for a cozier experience.

"This is absolutely amazing." She peered at the bookshelves nearest to her. "How are the titles organized?"

"It's better if you direct your questions to the librarian, Mr. Rhule." Evan paused. "Here he is now."

A translucent man, clad in a suit and tie fashionable decades prior, floated into view like a soap bubble. "May I help you find something, miss?"

Startled, Minna recoiled and grabbed Evan's arm.

"It's all right." The apprentice chuckled. "Miss Westerfield allow me to introduce you to our librarian, Mr. Rhule. He's a longtime employee who decided to stay on after he died. We'd be lost without him."

"But he's…he's…"

"Deader than a proverbial doornail." The librarian's smile was sanguine. "I'm not offended by the observation, I can assure you."

Minna gaped. "Are all the other employees at Harlequin Hall dead, too?"

"In that respect, I'm quite unique. I've no relatives I wanted to join in the hereafter, you see. Work always was my life and it's become my death, too."

Rendered speechless, she stared at the ghost, finding it difficult to focus on the apparition properly since everything behind him was visible.

Finally, she found her tongue. "Um…it's very nice to m-meet you."

He inclined his head. "Likewise. You were asking about the arrangement of our titles? It's alphabetical by author and arranged by section. Nonfiction on the gallery, and on this level, we have everything from classic literature to young adult fiction."

She blinked. "I've never seen so many books at one time."

"We have periodicals, too. And then there's the Tessellation Library."

"I've never heard of that."

"It's my own invention. Because I'm a spirit, I can bring you any book or periodical ever published from anywhere in the world, whether it's in this room or not." His eyes took on an extra gleam. "And I can do it almost instantaneously."

"Are you joking?"

Evan gave her a sidelong glance. "Test him, if you like. Mr. Rhule will produce anything you can think of."

Minna pondered the possibilities. "I-I'd like to see a yearbook from the Aldesbury Magic Academy, six years ago."

Evan scoffed. "That's too easy!"

"I want to remind myself what you looked like when you were twelve."

He laughed. "If you insist on going that route, I'd like to see a yearbook from Cardinal Hollow Secondary School, six years ago."

Mr. Rhule nodded. "Right away."

The ghost disappeared and Minna suddenly realized she was still gripping Evan's arm. She let go immediately.

"Sorry for grabbing you. It's just that I've never met a ghost before."

"Perfectly understandable. I admit, it took me aback the first time I met him as well."

When Mr. Rhule returned moments later, two books appeared on the display table at his elbow. "Here we are."

Minna scooped up the Academy yearbook with eager anticipation. "Thank you!"

She carried the book to the nearest seating area to look at the student portraits, and Evan did the same with the one from Cardinal Hollow Secondary School. Smiling up at her was the boy she remembered...although his hair had been cut more properly and combed for the photograph.

She tapped the image. "This makes me nostalgic. The day we met was the last normal day I had."

Evan gave her a sad smile. "I am sorry for everything that happened to you."

"Perhaps we can look forward to happier times in the future."

"Count on it." He held up her picture. "I remember this girl."

"Ooh, how dreadful!" She grimaced. "The day that picture

was taken, I had to get myself ready for school. My father was still in the hospital then, and my mother had gone to visit him. I tried to braid my hair the way my mother always did, but it ended up a mess. Fortunately, my teacher fixed it up for me."

"You were probably always the prettiest girl in school."

"No, but that's nice of you to say." She glanced at the Academy yearbook again. "Valentine is an unusual name."

Evan's smile faded. "I suppose it is, but I never had the chance to ask my father about it. He drank himself to death and I barely remember him at all." The wizard closed the yearbook with a snap and stood. "We should probably go."

Although Minna was somewhat taken aback at the rather terse rejoinder, she tried to shrug it off. She rose and glanced at the librarian, who was phasing in and out in a complicated pattern, as if to amuse himself.

"Thank you for your help, Mr. Rhule."

The ghost winked. "I'm always here."

Vibrations from his ghostly laugh sent a chilly wave down her spine, and she hastened to join Evan at the door. In contrast to his brusqueness only moments before, the young wizard now wore a cheerful smile.

As they crossed the entrance hall, she offered him a smile of apology. "I didn't mean to touch on a sore topic just now."

"A sore topic?" A blank expression crossed his face. "What are you talking about?"

"Your father."

"My father? He drank himself to death and I barely remember him at all." Evan gestured toward a pair of double doors. "Shall we go in?"

Minna was thoroughly perplexed at the exchange. Why had Evan repeated himself in such a strange fashion, almost as if he was reciting something from memory? Perhaps he'd been so estranged from his father, he didn't want to talk about him.

ALTHOUGH THE MEAL set in front of Minna looked and smelled delicious, she paid her food scant attention. Foremost in her mind was crossing the rift, locating Ned Rooney, and punishing him for what he'd done. Could she finally be close to achieving justice on behalf of the Westerfield family? Surely her father would forgive her for leaving once she told him why she'd really agreed to come.

Thaddeus glanced up from cutting into his freshly baked pudding. "If you don't care for roast beef, my dear, I'm sure the cook can make you something else."

"Oh, no, the food is wonderful."

"You're not unhappy with your room, I hope?"

She shook her head. "My room is perfect, thank you. Your great-granddaughter and I must have a great deal in common."

"That's quite true." Thaddeus turned to Evan. "You seem preoccupied this evening, lad."

"Er…indeed, yes. I'm sorry, sir. I don't mean to be dull company." Evan speared a chunk of roast beef into his mouth and chewed it.

The elderly wizard sighed. "Hmm. Well, perhaps the conversation should focus on our task tomorrow. Once we cross to the other side of the rift, the challenge will be to locate Ned Rooney. He could be anywhere by now, so it may prove tricky to find him."

"Not at all." Minna shook her head. "Finding Ned Rooney should be quite easy, I imagine."

"What makes you say that?" Evan asked.

"Tomorrow marks the opening of dragon racing season. A gambler like Ned Rooney will be at the track."

"Ha!" Thaddeus sat back with a gleeful grin. "Miss Westerfield, I *knew* you'd be an asset to this endeavor. We'll go straightaway after breakfast, and head to the stadium first."

A twinge of apprehension traveled down Minna's spine. "I can scarcely imagine crossing into another reality. Is it much different than this one?"

"Some things will be the same, and some not. There is simply no way to know until we get there," Thaddeus replied.

"You speak as if you've been to a different reality before."

The elderly wizard's eyes twinkled with mirth. "You don't suppose I would have invented a magical letter opener only to keep it in a drawer?"

Her mind raced. "Will we meet alternate versions of ourselves?"

"It's entirely possible. I often visit my counterparts in alternate realities. The old goats are devilishly hard to beat at chess."

The mental picture of Thaddeus as his own opponent struck Minna as incredibly funny, and she was seized with an attack of giggles. Her merriment was contagious, spreading to both Evan and Thaddeus.

Finally, the elderly wizard was obliged to wipe tears from his eyes. "I do love having young people around. I'm perfectly healthy, but at my age I can't help but think about my mortality. I hope after our little adventure with the rift, Miss Westerfield, you might consider staying on at Harlequin Hall—once we've squared things with your father, naturally."

"You're very kind, sir." She sought a topic to shift attention from her evasive response. "Forgive me if this is too personal, but I'd like to hear about your wife."

Evan's eyes widened at the personal question, but Thaddeus merely smiled. "Ah...my wife. I was married to an extraordinarily beautiful woman named Helena for over fifty years. After dinner, I'll introduce you."

Minna's jaw dropped. "Is she a ghost like Mr. Rhule?"

Thaddeus roared with laughter again. "I mean only to show you her portrait. Evan, will you please escort Miss Westerfield to my private study at nine o'clock sharp?"

"Sir?" Evan's brows shot upward and his look of surprise was almost comical. "We're invited to your inner sanctum?"

"Yes, indeed. There are some things I'd like to share with you both."

After he finished the main course, Thaddeus excused himself. "I'm going to enjoy a brandy in my study, but please stay for dessert. My cook has a touch of magical ability, so he always plans something special whenever we have guests."

Minna and Evan were left alone.

"Well done just now." He nodded toward Thaddeus's empty chair. "The old fellow has never seen fit to invite me to his study for a chat."

"Perhaps he was only waiting for the proper occasion."

"Perhaps. Timing is everything, so they say."

She cast about for a topic of conversation. "So, you were Valedictorian at the Academy, and now you're an apprentice to the most powerful wizard in recent history. Your family must be very proud."

"My mother is thrilled, naturally, but Uncle Joe is disappointed." He chuckled. "He bought the pub around the corner, and he wanted me to work for him. But I need to give my mother a comfortable life, and I can't do that working as a bartender."

"That's nice you want to provide for your mother."

"After all the sacrifices she's made for me, she deserves it."

A servant brought out individual lemon soufflés so light they hovered over the plate. Unfortunately, Minna had a difficult time pinning her soufflé down long enough to eat it. Her attempt to stick a fork in the confection sent it zooming across the table. Evan caught it before the dish hit the wall and sent it back to her.

"This is counter-intuitive, but you have to blow across the soufflé to make it stick to the plate," he said. "It's something about the puckering of the lips that calms the lemon."

"You're joking."

"Try it."

Minna blew across the soufflé. To her amazement, the pastry instantly dropped onto her plate. "How did you know to do that?"

"My mother manages a bakery, and occasionally I used food spells as a marketing gimmick."

She listened with fascination as he went on to describe the spells he'd used, such as spinning silver dragées, blooming rosebud icing, and glowing confetti decor.

"I could have done bigger spells with special event cakes, but the owner of the bakery said her clientele wouldn't be interested. It was a shame, too, because I'd devised a couple of rather complex spells I was eager to try. One involved sugar bells and music, and the other featured a light show."

"How clever!" Her heart suddenly felt more buoyant than the dessert. "I suppose you're used to it, but I can't tell you how wonderful it is to talk about magic without fear of anyone looking at me askance. What was it like to go to school at the Academy?"

"Fantastic. Intellectually stimulating. I was incredibly fortunate to attend."

She frowned. "I hear a 'but' in there somewhere."

"Well...I felt rather lonely upon occasion. I wasn't financially well off and I didn't want anyone to know. Everything I wore, including the uniforms, was secondhand. So I became rather good with glamour spells." He shrugged his shoulders. "I'm not sure anyone ever figured it out."

"I don't know much about glamour, but I've become very good at illusion spells. I couldn't let my father know I was studying magic. Every book I read, or any notes I wrote, took on the appearance of something else."

"I'm glad you've finally declared your independence, Miss Westerfield."

"Thank you. So am I." She paused. "Call me Minna."

"Only if you call me Evan."

"All right."

Her gaze lingered on his expensive-looking dinner jacket, but then she immediately focused on her soufflé. The question on her lips was one she had no business asking.

"Yes." Evan's voice was soft.

"What?"

"Everything I'm wearing and almost everything I own has been enchanted with a glamour spell. The stipend I earn with Mr. Bartholomew right now isn't enough to pay for the kind of clothes I'd like. After I pass my licensing exam, I'll make a better wage."

She felt her face heat with embarrassment. "I'm sorry. Was my curiosity that obvious?"

"No, but I thought I should be honest with you going forward. I haven't a penny to my name."

"We have that in common, then." She smiled. "Thank you for being so forthright."

As she finished her dessert, she wished she could be equally honest with Evan. If he suspected the depths of her hatred for Ned Rooney, however, he would refuse to let her anywhere near the man.

Thaddeus Bartholomew's study was accessible only by a private elevator tucked under one of the staircases in the entrance hall. After the elevator door closed, the carriage began to vibrate.

Minna frowned. "Are we moving up or down? I can't tell." A sudden change of direction sent her lurching into Evan's arms. "Oh, sorry!"

With a grin, he set her on her feet. "Sideways, it seems. I've never taken this elevator before, but it's magic. There's no telling where we'll stop."

She gripped one of the handrails for balance. After several more changes of direction, the doors opened to reveal the interior of a handsomely appointed railway carriage. Rows of seats were situation to either side, with a red-carpeted aisle down the middle.

Evan chuckled. "A train? This is novel."

"And quite elegant." She peered at the sunlit moors and languid waterways visible through the windows. "It's daytime, and we're moving."

"Obviously an illusion of some kind." Evan turned around just as the elevator doors transformed into the back window of a caboose. "This is an impressive bit of magic, even for Mr. Bartholomew."

"Indeed, it is, but there's no one here but us. I thought we were to join him in his study?"

He shrugged. "Let's work our way forward until we find him."

To Minna's surprise, the view visible from the next train carriage featured the glorious buttes, endless sand, and rock sculptures of a desert.

"What is this?" She gaped. "Does each railway carriage have a different view?"

"I don't know." Evan made a gesture of invitation. "Let's find out."

The landscape visible from the forward carriage resembled a rain forest, complete with waterfalls and exotic, colorful birds and flowers.

Minna smiled with pleasure. "I like this view best. It's so very tranquil."

"I would have termed it romantic."

"With a name like Valentine, you ought to be careful with that sort of comment. You could accidentally give a girl ideas."

She'd meant the remark to be teasing, but it came out as flirtatious.

Evan lifted one of his eyebrows. "Perhaps it wouldn't be accidental."

When she met his gaze, the atmosphere suddenly seemed thicker than it had moments before.

"You're not serious."

"Would that be a problem for you if I was?"

Her mouth went dry. "Y-You don't know me at all."

He moved closer. "I'd like to know you better, if you'd let me."

When Evan slid his arm around her waist, ripples of pleasure ran down her spine and made her nerves tingle.

"Do you feel that?" His lips hovered over hers. "It's the same sensation I felt when we first met."

"Yes." She wanted nothing more than to melt into him, but she fought to keep control. "I feel the same thing, but..." Minna gently disentangled herself and stepped away "...this isn't the time or the place. First, we must capture Ned Rooney."

"Ah. I almost forgot...timing is everything." He took a deep breath. "And Ned Rooney is just the topic to dampen my ardor."

She couldn't suppress a smile. "Sorry."

Evan returned her smile with a crooked grin of his own. "So we'll revisit this discussion after we have that reprobate sorted out?"

She averted her eyes. "If you still feel the same way about me."

"My intentions are unwavering." He glanced toward the forward door. "Shall we continue on?"

"Of course. I imagine Mr. Bartholomew is wondering where we are."

As Minna followed Evan down the aisle, she felt more than a little regret at putting him off. Despite Evan's sentiments at present, she doubted very much he'd want to deepen their relationship once he realized she'd used him to get her revenge. Her resolve weakened...but then she pushed her misgivings away. Ned Rooney had ruined her life and couldn't be allowed to escape vengeance, whatever the cost might be to her personally.

When she entered the next carriage, it seemed to be moving underwater like a submarine. As it passed through a coral reef, surrounded by colorful fish, Minna held her breath. Evan caught her eye and she realized he was holding his as well. They both burst into laughter and he grasped her hand.

"We should hurry before we pass out from lack of oxygen."

He pulled her along until they reached the last carriage, the windows of which were dark.

Evan peered at the windows with a frown. "We're in a tunnel."

"And we're out of train." She sank into a seat. "Perhaps we'll find Mr. Bartholomew when it stops."

Evan slid into the seat next to her, but moments later, the train pulled into a subway station.

He chuckled. "I guess we've arrived."

As they stepped from the train, Thaddeus met them with

an exasperated frown. "I thought you two would never take a seat! The train won't stop otherwise."

Evan cocked his head. "It would've been nice if you'd told us!"

"Where's the fun in that?" Thaddeus beckoned them forward. "Come into my study."

Minna and Evan followed him from the platform, glancing back to see a solid wall and a pair of elevator doors where the train had been moments before. Impressed, she shook her head in amazement.

"The train is an incredible illusion, Mr. Bartholomew."

His eyes twinkled. "What makes you think it's an illusion? It just so happens I love trains. If I hadn't been a wizard, I would have been a conductor."

The elderly wizard led her and Evan through a doorway and into his spacious study. The room was a blend of laboratory, library, and den. Over the mantelpiece hung a life-sized painting of a woman. Although the lady possessed a very beautiful face and figure, she also seemed reserved—perhaps even imperious. Her distinctive widow's peak reminded Minna of her mother and her great-aunt Bettina.

"Is the painting hanging over the fireplace of Mrs. Bartholomew?"

Thaddeus's expression as he glanced at the painting was a mixture of pride and sorrow.

"Indeed. In my youth, Helena Nancy Wimbleton was the most beautiful girl I ever beheld, and I wasted no time making her my wife. Helena was a strong wizard in her own right, a leader in aristocratic society, and mother to our five daughters. She was also a ruthless matriarch and had very specific ideas about which gentlemen would be proper matches for her girls. Helena saw our daughters married to rather stodgy, properly brought up gentlemen. When grandchildren came along,

Helena took it upon herself to ensure that they, too, made satisfactory matches." The elderly wizard turned toward Minna with a sad smile. "Unfortunately, our granddaughter, Nancy Minerva, had a mind of her own."

As he spoke, a prickling sensation at the back of Minna's neck became a buzzing in her head. "M-My mother's name was Nancy Minerva."

Mr. Bartholomew studied her a moment. "Yes, it was. She was my granddaughter."

Suddenly dizzy, Minna sank onto a footrest.

CHAPTER 6
COUNTERPART

"Are you all right, my dear?" Thaddeus conjured Minna a glass of water and pressed it into her hands. "You've grown rather pale."

She shook her head. "If you're my great-grandfather, why didn't you say anything before now?"

"I'd like an answer to that as well." Evan had taken a seat in a wing chair nearby and was staring at the elderly wizard as if he were a stranger. His gaze shifted to her. "Minna, please believe me when I say I'd no idea about any of this."

Thaddeus sighed. "You both deserve answers, but I'm not sure they will prove satisfying. Nevertheless, thank you for giving me the chance to explain."

He took off his spectacles to polish the lenses with a handkerchief, revealing brown eyes glistening with emotion. Even after he seemed to get his emotions under control, he was obliged to clear his throat several times before he could continue.

"Nancy Minerva had no talent for magic. Nevertheless, she was a stunning girl who made quite a splash in the society pages. My wife had high hopes she would marry into the aristocracy. You can't imagine Helena's dismay when Nancy eloped with a rising dragon jockey named Wynn Westerfield. It caused quite a scandal at the time, but my wife rectified the situation by systematically and methodically placing enchantments on her friends, family and even newspaper columnists until each one of us forgot Nancy ever existed."

Minna squeezed her eyes shut. "How ghastly."

"The only member of the family unaffected was my eldest daughter, who was so angry at Helena for cutting Nancy off that she refused to see her again."

"Great-Aunt Bettina."

Thaddeus nodded. "Helena passed away seven years ago without restoring my memory. Shortly thereafter, Wynn Westerfield had a horrendous accident. I followed the news like everyone else, of course, but I didn't realize any connection the Westerfield family had to me. You can imagine my bewilderment when Nancy Westerfield contacted me for help, claiming to be a relative. I sought Bettina's advice, and she discovered my memory had been altered."

Evan stirred. "How did she figure it out?"

"Memory alteration leaves a tell-tale clue in the rote recitation of a false narrative. Still, Helena would have succeeded in erasing Nancy altogether if it hadn't been for Bettina. My eldest daughter had always been fond of Nancy and assumed my lack of interest in her was due to Helena's influence. It *was*, in fact, but not in the way she'd imagined."

"No one should have the right to cast that sort of spell." Minna shot a cold glance at her great-grandmother's portrait. "It's unforgivable."

"I quite agree, my dear, and it's affected my regard for my late wife a great deal." Thaddeus frowned. "When Bettina managed to remove Helena's enchantment, I was devastated to realize I'd forgotten Nancy Minerva completely. Furthermore, I had a beautiful great-granddaughter I knew nothing about. Well, I set about to make amends as best as I could. Unfortunately, Wynn Westerfield was holding an implacable grudge against his wife's family as well as wizards, so Nancy Minerva forbid me from doing anything directly."

As suspicion dawned, Minna's eyes widened. "*You're* the one who set up that scholarship?"

"It was the least I could do."

Evan visibly flinched, but he said nothing.

Thaddeus continued. "I felt so distressed about missing your childhood that when your father refused the scholarship, I allowed the Academy to award it to another deserving child —one whose magical potential was quite out of the ordinary." His gaze rested on Evan. "That child has grown up to be my apprentice, and I'm quite proud of the way he turned out."

"Thank you, sir. I'm exceedingly grateful for your generosity." Despite Evan's sober expression, his lips quirked up at the corners. "If I hadn't attended the Academy, I'd be bartending for my uncle right now."

"And doubtless you would have been the best bartender anyone has ever seen." Thaddeus took a deep breath and let it out slowly. "I've no right to ask for your forgiveness, Minna, but I hope you'll allow this old man to be a part of your life going forward."

"There's nothing to forgive, Great-Grandfather."

"Call me Thaddeus, please. *Great-Grandfather* takes too long to say, and at my age I don't have time to waste."

Tears filled Minna's eyes as she stood and moved over to the elderly man. "I'd be honored to be part of your life, Thaddeus."

He embraced her with surprising strength. "Thank you. I explained some of this to your father before we left Cardinal

Hollow, but he has a great deal of understandable resentment to overcome. I shall endeavor to improve my relationship with him in the future."

Although Minna doubted such a thing was possible, she smiled and nodded. Perhaps when her father heard Thaddeus was responsible for leading her to Ned Rooney, his attitude would soften.

Her great-grandfather sank into a chair, looking every bit his age. "Now that we've had our chat, you two run along. We've got an important job to do tomorrow, so let's get some rest." He gestured toward a red leather upholstered door on the far wall. "Take that way back to the entrance hall. It's faster than the train."

Minna nodded. "Good night, Thaddeus."

"Good night, sir." Evan's tone sounded wooden.

The young wizard opened the door for her, and they passed through a short hallway until they emerged into the entrance hall. As soon as the door shut, it disappeared entirely.

"A one-way exit." Evan ran his fingertips over the now-smooth wall. "The old boy does everything with style."

"Indeed, he does."

As they began to climb the stairs to the upper level, his gaze flickered in her direction. "How are you doing?"

"As well as can be expected for a girl who just received shocking news." She shook her head. "I'm stunned."

"I can't imagine how you must be feeling." He studied her a moment. "I apologize for what I said earlier on the train, by the way. If I'd had any inkling who you were, I wouldn't have been so presumptuous."

She was taken aback. "So...you've changed your mind about me?"

"You're Mr. Bartholomew's great-granddaughter. He's my employer. Therefore, I should never have expressed my attraction to you." He shook his head. "Please don't give it another thought."

Although Minna had put Evan off before, she felt a surprisingly keen sense of disappointment.

"I see." When they reached the top of the stairs, she cleared her throat. "I don't want to be responsible for any awkwardness. After we finish our business with Ned Rooney, I'll go home. I can always arrange to visit Thaddeus some other time."

Evan frowned. "I don't want you to avoid Harlequin Hall because of me. Maybe I'll take a couple of weeks off instead, to cram for the licensing exam this fall."

"Were you planning to take a break before?"

"No, but—"

"Then that's out. Besides which, Papa and I have a great deal to discuss. He's probably terribly angry with me for deceiving him about studying magic."

Evan bristled. "Forgive me for saying so, but your father should have allowed you to attend the Academy."

"If he had, you couldn't have gone."

"The scholarship was rightfully yours." He shrugged. "I could have studied at home, same as you did."

"But you wouldn't have had Thaddeus's supervision." She sighed. "Please don't feel guilty. You earned that scholarship and have proven yourself worthy. I've only ever demonstrated how well I can hide."

"Ha!" Evan made a gesture with his fingers and suddenly the fabric of his clothes appeared worn, faded, and ill-fitting. The luster of his fair hair was slightly muted, and the perfect waves became a tousled mess. He spread his arms wide. "I've been hiding in plain sight for years."

Despite the self-mocking smile on Evan's lips, he'd never seemed more vulnerable...or irresistible.

"I see no great difference. You're just as handsome as ever."

His smile faded. "You really are magnificent, Minna Westerfield. Would you think me terribly forward if I asked you to be a friend?"

"I feel as if we already are."

They shook hands and parted company. As she began to climb the stairs to her tower, however, a draft made her shiver. Evan might approve of her at the moment, but tomorrow would change everything. Oh, why hadn't she let him kiss her before? At least then she'd always have the memory of his lips to keep her warm.

INNER TURMOIL and the frequent din of thunder prevented Evan from achieving a deep sleep. He'd carried a torch for Minna Westerfield for so long, he'd almost let it define him. Hiding his feelings going forward wouldn't be as easy as using a glamour spell. For Minna's sake, as well as his own, he'd have to manage it somehow.

As the night wore on, another worry occupied his thoughts. He was to locate Ned Rooney and recover the letter opener, yet suddenly he couldn't remember what the wizard looked like. Evan had read numerous newspaper stories about Rooney and watched his trial on the vidscreen, but for some reason the wizard's face was blank in his mind's eye. Evan tossed and turned as anxiety made it impossible to relax. He was apprenticed to the former Head Wizard of Ceresland, yet he couldn't visualize a simple target? The prospect of making an utter fool of himself in front of Minna and Thaddeus was not a pleasant thought.

He rose early and descended to the library, where Mr.

Rhule was hanging upside down from one of the chandeliers. Inexplicably, his head was wrapped in a towel.

"Mr. Rhule?"

The librarian couldn't hear him through the terrycloth, evidently, so Evan was reduced to waving his arms wildly until he drew his notice.

"Oh, hello Mr. Valentine!" The ghost unhooked his knees from the lighting fixture, floated to the floor, and lifted the towel to bare an ear. "How can I help you?"

Evan frowned. "What's with the towel?"

He shuddered. "The incessant thunder is vibrating my ectoplasm horribly. I feel as if I'm developing a spiritual rash."

"Hopefully the rift will be closed today, and you won't have to worry about it any longer. Um...can you bring me any newspaper articles with Ned Rooney's photograph?"

"Certainly."

Mr. Rhule drifted off and very shortly thereafter returned with an armful of periodicals. When Evan located Rooney's image, he was surprised to discover how poor his recollection had been. In his defense, nearly seven years had passed since the trial and Ned Rooney's features were scarcely distinctive.

Evan shook his head. "I'd forgotten what he looked like."

"Some faces are instantly forgettable." The librarian shrugged. "Oftentimes, that's a mercy."

The conversation reminded Evan of memory alteration spells.

"You must have read a great deal since your death, Mr. Rhule. Have you ever come across a charm to ward off a memory alteration spell?"

"Certainly! Just tie a string around your finger, and no such spell will stick."

Evan looked at him askance, but the librarian didn't appear

to be speaking in jest. "And…assuming it's too late for a charm, how would you remove such a spell?"

"Ah…well, that requires a potion known as a jog. It's brewed from an enchanted species of coffee bean and served over ice."

Evan peered at him. "You're pulling my leg."

"Why would I do that? I've always been dead serious." Mr. Rhule put his nose in the air and drifted off.

Minna entered the library. "Good morning. I thought I was the only early riser."

Evan stood as she crossed over to his table. "Good morning, Miss Westerfield…er, Minna." He gestured toward the newspapers. "I'm just doing some last-minute research."

"You, too?" She sighed. "I spent half the night here, looking up old newspaper stories about my mother when she was my age. She was a celebrity in her own right, yet she never said a word about it. I'm going to have my work cut out for me, trying to reverse my great-grandmother's mischief."

"Mr. Rhule says there's a potion you can use to counteract a memory alteration spell, but I'm not sure I believe him."

Minna rolled her eyes. "Yes, he told me about that potion last night with a straight face. The fellow has a unique sense of humor, I must say."

"He really *was* joking?" Since the librarian was absent, Evan was forced to scowl in the direction he'd seen him last. "The knave."

"There are no potions or charms in cases such as these. I called Aunt Bettina last night and she confirmed what Thaddeus told us; only the truth is an antidote."

"So how did she help your great-grandfather remove the alteration spell?"

"Aunt Bettina showed Thaddeus photographs of him with

my mother as she was growing up and he suddenly remembered her existence."

Evan frowned. "If I learned someone had used a memory alteration spell on me, I'm not sure I could control my temper. I'd be furious."

"Although Thaddeus hides his emotions well, I think he's still furious with Great-Grandmama. Since she's passed away, however, I don't imagine he'll ever get closure."

"You're his closure, I suspect."

Thaddeus's voice rang out from the entrance hall. "Good morning, children!"

"Good morning!" Minna hastened from the library.

Evan quickly tore Ned Rooney's picture out from the paper and stuffed it in his pocket. As he joined Minna in the entrance hall, Thaddeus came sailing down the railing on the seat of his trousers. Once he reached the newel post, he hopped off, chortling with glee.

"I should do that once a day to keep myself young." He linked arms with Minna and Evan. "Shall we see what gustatory delights the cook has prepared for us this fine morning?"

THE EXTENSIVE BUFFET included an egg dish, waffles, bacon, linked sausages, and wholesome oatmeal. Minna heaped her plate before joining Thaddeus and Evan at the table.

"I called Papa last night, to let him know I'd arrived." She slid into the chair opposite Evan. "I also called Aunt Bettina. She'd like to come for a visit. In fact, she insists."

"I think that's an excellent idea." Thaddeus spread open the napkin he'd tucked into his collar so as to spare his natty gold brocade vest. "We can begin rebuilding the Bartholomew family, one relative at a time."

Minna spread a pat of butter over her waffle. "I haven't seen Aunt Bettina since the funeral." As she reached for the small pitcher of hot syrup on the table in front of her, the heady fragrance of maple tickled her nostrils. "My great-aunt is almost a force of nature."

Evan sprinkled brown sugar over his oatmeal. "I'll look forward to meeting her."

The elderly wizard peered at him over the rims of his glasses. "You'll want to brace yourself."

Evan glanced from him to Minna. "That bad?"

Thaddeus cleared his throat. "Of all my daughters, Bettina was the most headstrong. I think she took after Helena." He consulted his pocket watch. "Tuck in, children. Time is running short."

A sudden surge of anxiety caused Minna's stomach to contract. Although she'd yearned for the moment she could mete out Ned Rooney's punishment, Thaddeus himself had mentioned the wizard's talent. The task at hand wouldn't be easy, and she'd be foolish to assume otherwise. She'd bloodied Rooney's nose before, admittedly, but he hadn't been expecting her attack back then. He'd be better prepared now, and likely looking over his shoulder whenever he was in public. Nevertheless, she had a few definite advantages. For one thing, she wasn't twelve years old any longer, and he wouldn't necessarily recognize her. More importantly, he didn't know she'd been studying magic under the tutelage of the former Head Wizard of Ceresland.

A slight smile lifted the corners of her lips and her nerves eased enough for her to continue eating her waffle. Considering the powerful trio of wizards preparing to embark on Rooney's trail, it was he who should be apprehensive, not her.

Evan glanced across the table. "You look as if you're enjoying your breakfast."

"Yes." She smiled. "Very much so."

A half hour later, Minna, Thaddeus, and Evan met in front of the infinity mirror, where Mr. Rhule was wringing his hands and wafting to and fro.

"Mr. Bartholomew, this constant thunder is making my death absolute purgatory. I urge you to complete your errand and close the rift just as soon as humanly possible."

"You're welcome to wait in my study, Mr. Rhule." Thaddeus gave him a sympathetic smile. "The only noise there is the soothing sound of the trains passing by."

"Thank you, sir, and Godspeed." Mr. Rhule drifted toward the elevator and disappeared through the doors.

Thaddeus rubbed his hands together as he regarded Minna and Evan. "Don't be apprehensive about entering the rift. Walking through the infinity mirror is as easy as Mr. Rhule walking through solid walls. I'll go first so you can see how it's done."

He lifted a foot high enough to clear the mirror frame, and then stepped through.

Evan exchanged a glance with Minna.

"Are you nervous?" she asked.

"A bit. You?"

"Terrified." She gulped. "This reminds me of evaluation day."

"Yes, I was scared to death until you gave me a kiss on the cheek. After that, I felt as if I could conquer anything." Evan offered her his hand. "Together?"

She took his hand and they stepped through the mirror at the same time. For a brief moment, the foamy sensation on her skin made her catch her breath. In the next moment, she and Evan were seemingly back where they'd begun.

"We're here, I guess." He shrugged.

Minna glanced around, confused. "But this reality is the same as the one we left."

Mr. Rhule sauntered over with a friendly smile. The librarian was clad in a dapper suit and by all indications was in the pink of health.

"Welcome, Miss Westerfield and Mr. Valentine. Both Mr. Bartholomews are in the drawing room, having a confabulation."

Minna gaped at him in amazement. "You're not dead!"

His eyebrows rose. "Most decidedly not. I don't even have a cold."

She blinked. "So...you know us?"

"Of course. Mr. Valentine came to work for Mr. Bartholomew not too long ago, and you and I have been well acquainted since I gave you piggyback rides through the library as a child."

Although she didn't want to be rude, she couldn't pretend to remember something that hadn't happened.

"Where I come from, you and I met just yesterday, I'm afraid."

He scratched his head. "So if I'm dead in your world, I must be some sort of zombie?"

"No, you're..." Minna trailed off, worried about offending him. "You're a ghost, actually."

From the amused expression on Mr. Rhule's face, he clearly thought she was speaking in jest.

"I'm a ghost, am I? You got me on that one, Miss Westerfield."

The man chuckled and shook his head as he disappeared into the library.

Evan lowered his voice. "I guess this reality isn't exactly the same as ours."

"Mr. Rhule's fortunes have improved, at least."

"Yes, in this world he's a snappy dresser and he breathes." He gestured toward the drawing room. "Shall we go speak with the dual Mr. Bartholomews?"

"Should be interesting."

Two elderly wizards were standing near the fireplace when Minna and Evan entered the room. Although they were identical in every other way, one wore a vest of blue brocade and his twin wore a vest of gold.

The blue brocade-clad wizard seemed startled to see them. "Are you back already?"

Thaddeus shook his head. "No, these two are with me."

Evan cocked his thumb over his shoulder. "We arrived through the infinity mirror, moments ago."

The first Thaddeus blinked. "What uncanny likenesses! My great-granddaughter wears her hair exactly like that." He paused. "I'm curious...are you two romantically involved in your reality as well as mine?"

Evan blurted out a reply. "We're just friends."

Minna blushed. "Very good friends."

"Oh, well, I don't mean to pry." The first Thaddeus chuckled. "Your entire future is yet unwritten."

The man in the gold vest beamed. "We'd love to stay longer, old boy, but we've a letter opener to retrieve and a criminal to catch."

His counterpart tossed him a set of car keys. "Your ride is parked out front."

Thaddeus caught the keys handily. "Thank you for the loan of a vehicle."

"I'm happy to help. And if you're anything like me—and I know you *are*—I'm certain you'll get your man."

Feeling awkward, Minna waved farewell to the elderly wizard. "It was nice to meet you, sir."

"You're welcome at Harlequin Hall, anytime."

Minna, Evan, and Thaddeus emerged from the castle and crossed the small bridge leading to the motor court. The stream and singing frogs were the same, but where the wolf had been before, a clay dragon was whistling counterpoint to the frogs' song of farewell.

"A whistling dragon! How charming," Thaddeus said.

Minna slipped Evan a sidelong glance. "Must be *my* counterpart's contribution."

He gave her a crooked grin. "When we return, you should replace the wolf with a dragon."

"I-I didn't mean to suggest the dragon was an improvement. I like the wolf, too."

"Truly, I prefer the dragon. It goes far better with the frogs."

Thaddeus cleared his throat. "I believe there's room for both." He held up the car keys. "Who'd like to drive?"

Parked in the motor court was a gleaming cherry-red convertible, built low to the ground.

Minna stared at the vehicle in admiration. "Isn't that gorgeous!"

Evan stared, his pupils fully dilated. "Oh, *yeah*." He held out his hand for the keys. "I'm driving, and it's not open for debate."

CHAPTER 7

ANOTHER PATH

Evan eased the flashy convertible into the long queue of personal vehicles and buses waiting to enter the Aldesbury Dragon Park car lot. Overhead, however, a diamond lane of personal dirigibles, antigrav buses, and airborne cycles zoomed into the elevated parking area, unimpeded.

The traffic jam made Evan shake his head in frustration. "Are we late? I didn't think the race started until noon."

"People arrive early to watch the pre-race exhibition. Jockeys take their dragons for a run beforehand to get excitement—and bets—flowing." As Minna spoke, her eyes were bright, and her color was high. "If we can ever get into the stadium, we'll find Rooney at the wagering windows."

"In that case, time is of the essence." Evan slid a finger alongside his nose. "Let's fly."

As the convertible floated into the diamond lane, Thaddeus hooted with laughter. "When did you learn to do this?"

"I learned from the best, sir."

Evan discovered the sports car handled just as well aerially as it had with its wheels on the road, and after he entered the elevated car lot, he pulled the vehicle into one of the plentiful parking ports.

"I love it when a challenge is successfully managed." The elderly wizard seemed uncommonly pleased. "Let's all remember where we parked!"

Evan attached the dock's bow and stern lines to the front and rear bumpers, and once the vehicle was secure, the three wizards made their way to a monorail station. As they rode the maglev train into the upper level of the stadium complex, he couldn't suppress a feeling of anticipation. Although his visit to Aldesbury Dragon Park was on serious business, he was thrilled to finally see the facility in person.

After the small party disembarked, Thaddeus pulled Minna and Evan aside. "If Ned recognizes me, he'll flee. Give me a moment while I don a disguise."

Before Minna or Evan could reply, Thaddeus transformed himself into a short, rotund gentleman, complete with a monocle and bowler hat.

"It's nice to see you again, Mr. Bodkins." Minna slid Evan an amused glance. "Evan, this is my supervisor from the Homeschooled Students for Sorcery Board of Education."

"Good one, sir." Evan patted his own stomach. "I would never have realized it was you underneath such a surfeit of illusion."

Thaddeus rubbed his hands together. "Excellent. Shall we search for Ned Rooney?"

"There are two banks of wagering windows on this level, one on either side of the stadium. I think we should split up to cover both of them," Minna suggested. "He'll have to show up sooner or later to place his bets."

"You two check out the windows on the north side and I'll take the south," Thaddeus said. "If you find Ned, immobilize him with a binding spell and search him for that letter opener."

EVAN AND MINNA squeezed through the crowded corridor on their way to the wagering windows. Just as she'd said, dragon jockey exhibitions were underway in the stadium, and the spectators in the stands were making their enthusiasm known. An announcer and color commentator kept a fairly constant stream of chatter flowing over the speakers, and smaller vidscreens were positioned at regular intervals so concession-goers and gamblers wouldn't miss the action taking place on the track.

He raised his voice to be heard over the noise. "I can barely hear myself think!"

Minna grinned. "I know! Don't you find it exciting?"

"Maybe under different circumstances I would." Evan slipped the newspaper photograph from his pocket. "With all this commotion, I can't seem to fix Rooney's image in my mind."

"Don't worry, I'll recognize him for you. The man is—"

Minna broke off as the color commentator announced the next incoming team. Her face grew pale, and her head whipped toward the small vidscreen. Wynn Westerfield had entered the stadium and was flying toward the central platform on My Girl. The crowd was stamping their feet and cheering with such enthusiasm, it sounded as if the stadium were inside a tornado.

Evan struggled to keep up when Minna darted through the short tunnel into the stands. They joined the throng of onlookers at the railing just as Wynn Westerfield and My Girl streaked past. To the delight of everyone in the stadium, the dragon jockey put his mount through several fancy aerial maneuvers before bringing the exquisite coppery-golden dragon in for a landing. Minna's knuckles showed white as she gripped the top of the metal fence.

Evan peered at her. "Are you all right?"

"My father is still racing." She shook her head in amazement. "The accident never happened here."

She started to dart away, but Evan grabbed her by the elbow. "Where are you going?"

"My father will be returning to his dressing room soon, and he'll stay there until race time. I have to see him."

"That man isn't your father, Minna, and we have a job to do."

She pulled away. "I don't care. I'm going to see him whole again, up close. You can come with me—or you can stay here."

Without waiting for an answer, she hastened from the stands. In Evan's firm opinion, nothing good would come from dwelling on what could have been. From the set expression on Minna's face, however, he realized arguing with her would make no difference. Left with no choice, he accompanied her to a service elevator.

As the elevator descended into the bowels of the stadium, Minna fidgeted impatiently.

"I'll bet you anything Crucible is My Girl's sire."

He didn't bother to say that the dragons in this reality were unrelated to the ones at home. Although Minna knew better, she was clearly in no mood to listen to reason. A few moments later, they stepped out into a huge corridor, where a surly security wizard greeted them with a clipboard and a scowl.

"No fans allowed down here unless you're on the list. Please return to the elevator before I have you escorted from the stadium."

Evan bristled, but Minna just smiled. "I'm Wynn Westerfield's daughter, Minna. I'm on the list."

The wizard consulted his clipboard. "You're cleared, but you're not allowed any guests."

Minna grabbed Evan's hand. "This is my boyfriend, Evan Valentine."

The wizard was obviously unimpressed. "I don't care if he's gum sticking to the bottom of your shoe. If he's not on the list, he's not permitted to be on this level."

Evan's eyes narrowed. "You're horribly rude. I demand to speak with your supervisor—"

Wynn Westerfield's voice boomed down the hallway. "Minna! I didn't expect you today but come on back. You too, Evan."

Minna hurtled down the hallway and into his arms. "Papa!"

Evan shot the security wizard a nasty look before he brushed past. "The name's Evan Valentine." He pointed at the clipboard. "Write it down so you don't forget."

As he joined Minna and Wynn, he gave the jockey a nod. "That was some fancy flying out there, Mr. Westerfield."

To his surprise, Wynn pulled him into a backslapping man hug. "Good to see you, lad! I trust you're treating my daughter right?"

"Er…yes sir." At the last moment, Evan recalled he and Minna were supposed to be a couple. "I'm a lucky wizard."

"That you are."

Wynn ushered them into his dressing room, where the walls were covered with portraits of him alongside his winning mounts. An impressive floating floral arrangement filled the far corner, and a comfortable seating area gave the space a luxurious, comfortable feel.

Minna wrapped her arms around Wynn's waist in another tearful embrace and the dragon jockey's eyebrows lifted.

"What's this about, sweetheart?" He gave her a puzzled frown. "Has something happened?"

Minna stepped back, brushing moisture from the corners of her eyes. "It's just...you look so healthy and vibrant, Papa. It makes me happy to see you this way."

"Does some gossip columnist have me at death's door?" He chuckled. "I can assure you, I've never felt better."

A stunning older brunette entered the dressing room, clad in chic apparel and accompanied by a cloud of delicate perfume. Evan gaped at her elegance and beauty, but she just smiled and patted him on the cheek.

"What a lovely surprise, Evan! I thought my grandfather sent you and Minna off hunting dangerous magical artifacts in a ghastly foreign crypt."

Minna stared at Nancy Masters Westerfield, tears spilling down her face. "Mama!"

Evan found moisture stinging his own eyes as she pulled her mother into a hug.

"What's wrong, pumpkin?" Nancy exchanged a worried glance with her husband.

Wynn shrugged. "I suspect our daughter read some lies about my health in one of the papers. I'm going to have to speak to my publicist about it. I don't want these reporters scaring the wits out of my family."

Sobbing brokenly, Minna could only shake her head. Evan cast about for some excuse he could give to explain her emotional state.

"Um...there's no newspaper story of which I'm aware." He braced himself. "Minna's a bit emotional today because, uh...I asked her to marry me." When she stared at him in obvious shock, Evan hoped he hadn't said the wrong thing. "She turned me down, of course."

Wynn gave him a sympathetic glance. "I'm sorry for you, lad, but you seem to be taking it awfully well…better than my daughter, at any rate."

"Minna was concerned about losing my friendship, but I told her there was no reason to worry."

Nancy put a comforting arm around Minna's shoulders. "There's no reason to be upset, sweetheart, but you've made the right choice. You and Evan are simply too young for that sort of commitment."

"Yes, and that's why I refused." Minna grabbed a tissue from a nearby table and wiped her eyes. "Evan was sweet to propose, but I need more time."

"Timing is everything." He gave her a little wink.

She smiled through her tears. "Let's not mention the proposal again, shall we? I want to take things a bit slower."

"I won't say a word, especially not to Mr. Bartholomew." Evan grimaced. "If he knew I'd made you cry, he might transform me into a frog."

Nancy waved a dismissive hand. "Grandpapa wouldn't dream of doing anything so vulgar!"

Evan chuckled. "I should hope not."

Minna took a deep breath. "Well, we're on duty, so I suppose we should get going."

"Best of luck in the race today, sir." Evan nodded at Wynn. "You're in fine form."

"Thank you, lad."

Nancy smiled. "Give our best to your parents, Evan."

He froze. "Y-You've met my parents?"

"We attended the graduation ceremony together, don't you recall?" She gestured toward one of the photographs hanging on the wall behind him. "I just had that framed."

As Nancy talked with Wynn about the interviews he had scheduled after the race, Evan turned to get a better look at the newly framed photograph. The image showed him and Minna in their Aldesbury Magic Academy graduation caps and gowns, flanked on either side by two sets of parents. As he peered at the photo in disbelief, something clicked in his brain and a fog lifted. Betrayal ensued, followed by white-hot anger.

"Excuse me, Minna. I just remembered there's something I need to do." With fists balled at his side, he strode from the dressing room without a backward glance.

THE HAIR on Minna's forearms prickled as Evan left and a wave of apprehension ensued. The expression on his handsome face —at once cold and yet enraged—reminded her of how she'd felt that day in the courtroom when Ned Rooney had been sentenced. She hastened over to the photograph to see what had upset him...and gasped. A beaming older wizard had a proud hand on his son's shoulder and his arm around Mrs. Valentine's waist.

Ned Rooney is Evan's father.

Although she fervently wished it weren't so, her conclusion was unmistakable. Certain events in this reality weren't exactly the same as in hers, admittedly, but the people appeared to be identical. From Evan's shocked reaction to the photograph, he'd had no idea of his actual parentage...but it was worse than that.

Memory alteration leaves a tell-tale clue in the rote recitation of a false narrative.

When she'd asked Evan about his father, he'd repeated the same story in the exact same language. Further, he'd had difficulty recalling what Ned Rooney looked like. If truth was an antidote to memory alteration, obviously this photograph had obliterated the spell cast by his own father.

If I learned someone had used a memory spell on me, I'm not sure I could control my temper. I'd be furious.

Yes, she recognized Evan's virulent expression full well since she'd harbored the same hatred in her heart for years. He was bent on revenge, but if he succeeded in hurting Ned Rooney, his relationship with Thaddeus would be forever damaged. She must find a way to stop Evan before he ruined his life, even if that meant protecting the wizard who'd ruined hers. The irony tasted bitter, but her feelings for Evan made her choice clear.

Minna edged toward the door. "Good luck in the race today, Papa. I know you'll win."

His smile was warm, and his eyes crinkled at the edges. "Thank you, sweetheart."

With one last, lingering glance at the people who resembled her parents, she spun on her heel, dashed into the corridor, and sped toward the service elevator. The security wizard was inexplicably frozen in place—presumably the victim of Evan's ire. After she removed whatever spell had immobilized him, the man flinched in surprise.

"Where did you come from?"

She gave him an apologetic smile. "Sorry, I didn't mean to startle you."

As she punched the elevator call button, the wizard rubbed his eyes.

"That was weird. One second, I'm looking at your boyfriend, and the next, I'm looking at you."

She bit her lip. "You probably zoned out for a minute."

"Yeah, that must be it. Either that, or Valentine put a spell on me."

"Ha!" Minna feigned amusement. "Not likely."

When the door slid open, she hastened inside the elevator and pressed the uppermost button. Evan would probably start searching the wagering windows on the top level of the stadium and work his way down. She had to stop him before he found his father.

As soon as Evan stepped off the elevator, he sent a rolling spell out in all directions to immobilize everyone in sight. The use of such magic against strangers without their consent was forbidden, but he was past caring. After a lifetime believing his father had died from alcoholism, the realization he'd been duped was a bitter pill to swallow. Ned had magically altered his memory—and probably those of his mother and uncle—so he could abandon his family with impunity. Now it was time for the man to pay the price.

Evan mounted a stone bench so he could survey the crowd. Fortunately, he had no trouble remembering his father's most recent image from the graduation photograph hanging in Wynn Westerfield's dressing room. The happiness represented in that picture stuck in his craw especially. His counterpart in this reality had grown up with a father who loved him and had been proud of his accomplishments, whereas Ned had escaped all family obligations in favor of gambling and vice.

Finally, he spied the older man queued up at one of the wagering windows. He leaped off the bench and darted around motionless people as he approached his quarry. Ned Rooney—Ned Valentine, actually—was just turning away from the window with his ticket in hand. A muscle worked in Evan's jaw as he searched the man's pockets for the letter opener. When he finally located the slender length of metal in a sheath strapped to Ned's ankle, he held it up for closer examination.

Considering that it belonged to Thaddeus, he wasn't surprised to discover the slender pewter blade was topped by a jumping speckled frog. He slid the opener into his belt...and allowed the palms of his hands to fill with flames. Should he light Ned's hair on fire first or the cuffs of his trousers before lifting the immobilizing spell?

"Stop!" Minna appeared at his elbow. "Listen to me, Evan. I only came with you and Thaddeus to find Ned Rooney and hurt him for what he did."

As Evan stared at her, the flames in his hands ebbed. "Are you saying you want a shot at him first?"

"No, I'm telling you I've changed my mind. I've come to realize if I allow hatred to shrivel my soul, Ned will have truly succeeded in ruining my life." She shook her head. "I don't want that for myself...or for you."

His eyes narrowed. "You've every right to see my father suffer. He deserves it for what he did to your family."

"Yes, but it's not worth the cost." Minna moved closer. "Until you arrived at my door with Beast, I had nothing but hate in my heart. Because of you, I'm now ready to let my vendetta go." She melted into his arms. "I'd rather have a relationship with Evan Valentine than punish his father."

Evan squeezed his eyes shut as he held her tight, allowing the delicious sensations her proximity aroused to calm the raging anger within him. A wellspring of emotion overflowed, and his bitterness was replaced by tenderness, yearning—and relief.

"Ned Rooney's my father, Minna. How can you ever forget that?"

"It's simple. You're a good, kind man with talent most wizards can't possibly imagine." She pulled back to meet his gaze. "If you don't throw away a bright future in favor of revenge, neither will I."

She lifted up on her tiptoes to press a gentle kiss to his lips, and Evan felt his body warming with a far more pleasurable sort of flame than before. After he returned her kiss with one of his own, he inhaled deeply and allowed his shoulders to relax.

"I have the letter opener. Let's track down Mr. Bartholomew and tell him we've captured Ned. He can decide what to do with him."

Minna smiled. "Agreed."

"Bravo." Thaddeus stood where Ned Rooney had been moments before. "Well done, both of you."

As her great-grandfather revealed himself, Minna's jaw dropped in shock. "What's going on here, Thaddeus? Are you playing some kind of joke?"

"It's no joking matter. You've just been through a very serious wizarding ordeal, which you've both passed."

Evan was pale. "Do you mean to say you didn't trust me?"

"I never doubted you, lad. Once you discovered your father's betrayal, however, I knew you'd be furious." The elderly wizard put his hand on Evan's shoulder. "You needed to confront your rage, but now you know you can trust yourself to do the right and proper thing, despite temptation to the contrary."

"Only because of Minna. She convinced me to calm down."

"Considering her own grievances, I'm impressed she managed to persuade you." Thaddeus nodded. "You and my great-granddaughter make a good team."

Minna frowned. "How could you know I meant to seek revenge?"

"You wouldn't be human if you didn't feel resentful toward

Rooney, but I hoped you would ultimately choose another path. I was not disappointed."

"Hang on." Clearly bewildered, Evan stood with his arms akimbo. "If *you're* here, where is my father?"

Thaddeus wore a sheepish expression. "In prison, back in our dimension. I captured him personally a few days ago, but it hasn't hit the newspapers yet." His faded brown eyes regarded Minna and Evan with affection. "Forgive me for my subterfuge, but you both had unresolved issues to overcome, and I felt as if this exercise was the best way to go about it."

Evan gaped. "How long have you known about Ned's memory alteration spell?"

"I became aware of it only recently. Ned and I had a long talk after I captured him, you see." Thaddeus's ordinarily jovial expression became grim. "I made him rather, well, *uncomfortable* until he confessed everything."

Minna folded her arms across her chest. "Good."

"Nevertheless, sir, you took a horrible risk!" Evan bristled. "I could have burned you to death!"

"But you didn't."

Evan pulled the letter opener from his belt. "And is this just some kind of stupid prop?"

"Not at all." Thaddeus remained sanguine. "It's a valuable family heirloom, so I'll have it back now."

He took the opener from Evan and returned it to his ankle sheath.

"What about the electrical storms back home?" Minna cocked her head. "Don't tell me they were a ruse too?"

"In a way, but the storms weren't of my making. They were a bit of mischief Ned unleashed to cover his escape from prison. They'll likely be gone by the time we return, but he's to be charged with the malicious discharge of destructive magic." Thaddeus glanced at Evan. "Speaking of which, if you'll release all these good people, Mr. Valentine, I'll forget about your illegal use of a spell without consent."

"Sorry about that." Evan lifted his spell and people sprang to life, oblivious to what had gone on before.

Thaddeus rubbed his hands together. "Since we're here, and since the race is about to begin, shall we watch the Dragon National? I'll order hot dogs and all the trimmings delivered to my box. Well, the box belongs to my counterpart, but I know he won't mind."

The elderly wizard gestured for them to follow as he made his way to the stairs. Evan stood firm until Minna slipped her hand in his.

"You're upset, I can tell."

He was trembling. "I could have killed that wizard, and all he wants to do is eat hot dogs?"

"Thaddeus trusted you and me to do the right thing." She tugged him forward. "Let's go watch the race. My mother will probably be there."

His voice grew gentle. "The Nancy Westerfield in this reality isn't your mother."

"I know, but she makes me feel...whole again somehow."

"I understand completely." Evan pulled her into an embrace and kissed her. "You make me feel whole again."

CHAPTER 8
A WIZARD'S SOLUTION

As Thaddeus, Nancy Westerfield, and the two young wizards watched from a private box overlooking the stadium, Wynn Westerfield won the Dragon National in a spectacular finish.

"I must admit, watching the race in person was a lot more exciting than I had anticipated." Evan's voice was husky from cheering. "Wynn Westerfield is truly an amazing athlete."

Minna gave Nancy a hug. "I never had any doubt Papa would win!"

"Nor did I, but Wynn never takes anything for granted. He trained just as hard for this race as he did for his very first one, twenty years ago." Nancy smiled at Thaddeus. "I'm glad you and your apprentices could put your business aside long enough to join me!"

He beamed. "As it so happens, these two managed the task admirably."

Nancy gathered her handbag and wrap. "If you'll excuse me, I must meet Wynn in his dressing room to help him deal with reporters." She blew a kiss to Minna, Evan, and Thaddeus. "See you soon!"

Minna smiled. "Good-bye, Mama. I wouldn't have missed today for anything."

Nancy hastened from the box, and Thaddeus finished off the last bite of his hot dog.

"I adore hot dogs. Unfortunately, my cook thinks they're beneath him." He wiped mustard from his mustache and produced a slip of paper from his pocket. "Give me a few minutes while I cash in my winning ticket, will you?"

Evan looked at him askance. "I can't believe you really wagered on the Dragon National."

"I had to remain in character, didn't I? It's just happenstance I bet on the winner." He chuckled to himself on the way out.

Evan waited to speak until he and Minna were alone. "I'm still a trifle annoyed at being played. How can I ever trust him again?"

Her expression grew pensive. "I *should* be angry with him, but I'm not. I truly believe Thaddeus wants the best for us."

"But..." Evan made a sound of disgust as Ned Valentine appeared. "Oh, not this again!"

"Hello, lad!" The older man cocked his thumb over one shoulder. "I just ran into Mr. Bartholomew outside and he told me you were here. Congratulations on your father's triumph, Miss Westerfield." He waved a ticket. "I confess, I bet a great deal of money on him."

Evan sighed. "Do you think we're stupid enough to fall for the same ruse twice?"

A puzzled expression passed over Ned's face.

"Your mother knows I'm here, if that's what you're worried about."

Minna shot Evan a warning glance. "I'm afraid Evan is

mixed up from a little practical joke my great-grandfather played on him earlier. It has nothing to do with you, Mr. Valentine."

"I see." The older man's frown disappeared. "That's a relief!"

Taken aback by his mistake, Evan felt a blush warming his cheeks. "Sorry about that, er, Father. I didn't mean to be rude."

"No problem at all. I'm sure being apprenticed to the former Head Wizard of Ceresland keeps you on your toes."

"Y-Yes. Yes, it does."

Ned grinned. "I'm proud of you, son, and wouldn't be at all surprised if you become the youngest Head Wizard in Ceresland history." His gaze slid to Minna. "I hope you don't mind my bragging on him a bit."

"Of course not. I'm proud of him, too."

Evan's throat tightened at the praise, and he was unable to respond. Fortunately, Minna came to his rescue.

"If we'd realized you were at the stadium, Mr. Valentine, we would have asked you to join us. As you see, my great-grandfather had plenty of room in his box."

"Perhaps next time." Ned lifted his hat. "Give my best wishes to your parents, Minna."

"I will, thanks."

He winked at Evan before ducking out of the box. Overcome with emotion, Evan sank down in a seat.

Minna sat down next to him. "Are you all right?"

"Hearing my father say he was proud of me was something I never expected."

She gave him a soft smile. "That man isn't actually your father."

"I know, but he could have been." He swallowed hard. "And what he said meant...everything to me."

Minna rested her head on Evan's shoulder. "Believe me, I understand completely."

~

EVAN, Minna, and the two Thaddeus Bartholomews gathered in front of the infinity mirror as they prepared to step through to their own reality.

Evan handed the car keys to Thaddeus's counterpart. "You have a very sweet ride, Mr. Bartholomew. Thanks for the loan."

The wizard's eyes danced. "Actually, the convertible belongs to *my* Evan Valentine. I knew he wouldn't mind if I loaned it to you."

"He owns that car?" Evan slid a hopeful glance to *his* Thaddeus. "Do you suppose I could drive something like—"

"Don't even think about it." The elderly wizard waved off the implied suggestion with a chuckle. "One man's reality is another man's pipe dream."

Evan shrugged. "Oh, well. I have something to strive for."

Thaddeus gave his counterpart a wink. "I'll see you soon for that rematch."

The elderly wizard laughed. "And I'll look forward to trouncing you!"

Thaddeus Bartholomew touched the brim of his hat before stepping into the rift, and Minna and Evan followed. The transparent appearance of the ghostly Mr. Rhule moments later reassured Minna that they'd returned to their own reality.

"Back so soon?" Mr. Rhule asked.

"I thought you were going to wait in Thaddeus's study?" Minna asked.

"And so I did, but the thunder passed." He sighed. "I was looking forward to a little dead time."

The ghost disappeared into the library as Thaddeus sealed the infinity mirror with a spell.

"And that's that. Tomorrow, however, we have another monumental challenge to overcome."

"Which is?" Evan asked.

Thaddeus winced. "Wynn Westerfield. His resentment of me will be extraordinarily difficult to overcome, I fear."

A stab of apprehension made Evan's stomach contract. "I'm sure he has no great admiration for me, either."

Minna frowned. "Aunt Bettina will be arriving at Harlequin Hall before dinner tonight. I'll ask her to join us when we drive to Cardinal Hollow. Surely she'll be able to talk sense into Papa...if anyone can."

"Good idea." Thaddeus nodded. "We need all the reinforcements we can get."

ONCE THE LIMOUSINE passed the roadside sign for Cardinal Hollow, Minna gave the woman sitting next to her a nervous smile.

"We're nearly there."

Aunt Bettina gave her a pat on the hand. "Gird your loins, dear. And remember, you're a dragon rider's daughter as well as a wizard!"

"I'm girding." Minna exchanged an amused glance with Evan in the rear-view mirror.

Thaddeus waved a finger in the air. "Think not of battle, but of détente."

Evan's chuckle sounded slightly forced. "I believe I'll gird my loins, just in case. A wizard can never be too cautious."

Very shortly thereafter, the vehicle pulled up to the Westerfield house, and its occupants disembarked. As Minna climbed the front porch stairs, she could hear Beast barking madly on the far side of the door.

"Our arrival can scarcely be a surprise now."

Her father opened the door before she touched the handle. The small black puppy ran out to greet Minna, while the tall dragon jockey blocked the entrance.

"Thank you for returning my daughter." He delivered the statement with a scowl. "Good day to you."

Aunt Bettina stepped into view. "You're just as pig-headed as you ever were, Wynn Westerfield!" She climbed the steps and shook her walking stick in his face. "How my niece tolerated it, I'll never know, but Nancy swore there was some good in you."

His eyebrows rose. "Hello, Aunt Bettina."

"We're all going to go into the house, sit down like civilized people, and hammer this out." She wedged her walking stick in between Wynn and the door, levered him aside, and gestured toward Thaddeus and Evan. "Come along."

The two men followed her inside, leaving Minna and her father on the porch.

He gave her a level glance. "Is this some sort of ambush?"

Minna winced. "No. It's more like an intervention."

She picked up Beast and preceded her father into the house. While Evan held the puppy, she assembled a tray of refreshments from the kitchen. With little reason to hide her magical abilities any longer, the task took no longer than a minute.

Aunt Bettina took a sip of tea and grimaced. "This is disgusting. Have you a splash of brandy?"

"I'll bring you some." Minna stifled a smile as she went to fetch the bottle.

When everyone was settled with their choice of coffee or tea—spiked or otherwise—Thaddeus took the floor and repeated the story he'd related to Evan and Minna in his study.

Wynn shook his head. "Except for Aunt Bettina, Nancy's family shunned her all these years. Now you expect me to believe some nonsense about a memory alteration spell being responsible?"

"It's not nonsense, I'm afraid. Mama had a terribly vindictive, controlling streak in her." Aunt Bettina frowned. "Any apology I could offer would be wholly inadequate."

"Memory alteration spells are uncommon, I think, but I was the victim of one as well." Evan's spine straightened. "In fact, yesterday I discovered I'm related to Ned Rooney. You should know he's my father, Mr. Westerfield."

Minna gasped at Evan's honesty and courage, but Wynn's eyes turned steely.

"How *dare* you come into my house?" He drew himself up to his full height with his hands curled into fists at his side. "Get out before I throw you out!"

When Evan shot to his feet, Beast whined and dove under a chair.

"I didn't know who Ned Rooney was, Mr. Westerfield. Furthermore, I have every reason to despise him." The young wizard spoke without any trace of combativeness, however the set of his jaw demonstrated a refusal to be intimidated. "He abandoned me and my mother when I was very young."

Wynn swelled with umbrage. "Why should I believe the son of convicted wizard?"

Aunt Bettina tapped her walking stick on the floor. "Sit down, both of you!"

To Minna's surprise, the two men sat instantly—as if a tall giant had pushed them down by their shoulders. She'd had no idea her great-aunt was such a powerful wizard.

"Evan is telling the truth." Thaddeus cleared his throat.

"When I returned Ned Rooney to prison, I interrogated him personally. He deceived his own family as to his existence, and young Mr. Valentine has no relationship with the man whatsoever."

Minna fixed her father with an impassioned glance. "Furthermore, Evan Valentine is hard working, kind, and wickedly talented. I care about him very much."

Aunt Bettina lifted her teacup. "Wynn, it sounds as if you and young Mr. Valentine have a great deal in common."

"Especially when it comes to Minna." Evan's color was high. "I'd do anything for her."

"Well, well, well." Grim-faced, Wynn folded his arms across his chest as his cool glare slid from Evan to Minna. "I'm learning quite a few secrets today."

"Oh heavens, Minna has grown up and met a boy!" Aunt Bettina waved her hands in the air in mock outrage. "Who would have guessed?"

"Papa, my regard for Evan is not a secret, and it's not new." Minna held her father's gaze. "I've felt the same way about him ever since we met as children."

"Wynn, my great-granddaughter is an extraordinarily gifted wizard as well as a lovely young lady. I've asked her to be my apprentice along with Evan," Thaddeus said.

Minna's father grew pale. "You can't do that! She's all I have left."

Aunt Bettina made a sound of disgust. "She needs to be out on her own. She can't live her life for you."

Wynn's expression softened as he regarded his daughter. "Is this what you want?"

"More than anything." Minna swallowed hard. "But I don't want you to be unhappy or lonely, either."

"I didn't come to take her away and give nothing in return," Thaddeus said. "It just so happens, when I conferred with my wizard counterpart in another dimension, he offered me a potion to heal your injuries."

"I don't want any *wizard's* help, whatever it might be." A muscle rippled in Wynn's jaw. "I don't need any help at all."

"Oh, stow it, lad! You make my head hurt." Aunt Bettina poured another splash of brandy in her teacup.

Minna knelt at her father's knee. "If you won't let Thaddeus heal your arm, I can do it. You can have your racing career back, Papa."

He frowned. "That's impossible. Even if my arm were in perfect condition, I'm too old to race."

Evan cleared his throat. "That's not the case, sir. Mr. Bartholomew, Minna, and I just watched your counterpart in another world win the Dragon National." A smile curved his lips. "And he did it with your customary style and panache."

"I don't believe you."

"Wait a moment..." Thaddeus began to search his jacket pockets, and finally produced a slip of paper. "Here's my winning ticket, showing my bet. Wynn Westerfield on My Girl." He gave Minna's father the stub. "You see? The date was yesterday."

A myriad of emotions crossed Wynn's handsome face as he stared at the ticket. "If...if I could only fly a dragon once again, that would be something."

Aunt Bettina poured brandy in his teacup. "Drink this down and let your wizard daughter heal your injuries. If she can improve your disposition in the bargain, that would be a public service."

Minna gave her father an encouraging smile. "Trust me for once. If Mama were here, she would want me to help."

Beast wiggled out from his hiding place and scampered over to Wynn. He stood on his hind legs, put his paws on the dragon jockey's knee, and wagged his tail.

"Even the dog is begging you to cooperate." Aunt Bettina guffawed. "I'd take that as a sign."

Wynn muttered, "Hocus-pocus nonsense," but he unbuttoned his shirt and peeled it off.

When Minna saw the scars marring her father's imposing physique, she found it difficult not to hold back tears. The skin on Wynn's arm had been withered and melted by dragon fire so badly his range of motion was extremely limited.

Thaddeus retrieved a small, glass bottle from his pocket and uncorked the top. "Rub this potion into your hands, Minna. As long as the light lasts, it will allow you to heal any injury you touch."

Minna cupped her hands together. "I'm ready."

Her great-grandfather poured out a sky-blue waterfall into her hands. Once her palms and fingertips were glowing with gentle light, she traced over her father's scars. The shiny, puckered skin softened, and the angry red color faded to a more normal pink. The tissue gradually returned to a healthier condition until she was satisfied nothing more could be done.

"I think that's all the healing we can expect, Papa. Your arm may always look like you have a slight sunburn, but you should be able to move it far better now."

Stunned, Wynn stretched and flexed his arm. "I haven't been able to do this in years."

"Beautifully done, Minna." Bettina beckoned her over. "While you're at it, deary, I could use some help with my bursitis." The elderly woman stuck out her bony knee. "As far as healing spells go, I could never manage more than a wart removal charm."

A newly limber Aunt Bettina volunteered to make sandwiches for the road. The elderly woman was humming under her breath in the kitchen when Minna left to pack a battered trunk with her possessions.

As she worked, she heard the murmur of voices in the living room. Although the conversation between her father, Evan, and Thaddeus seemed civil enough, she was worried nevertheless until she heard Evan laugh.

A few minutes later, he joined her. "Mr. Bartholomew invited your father to drive back to Harlequin Hall with us."

Minna frowned. "That would be wonderful, but the limo only holds four people."

"Mr. Bartholomew said the car can magically expand to hold as many people as necessary. That's why it's called a stretch limo." He winked.

She giggled. "In that case, I hope Papa agreed to come."

Evan nodded. "He's agreed to visit, but not for a few days. He wants to set up meetings with possible sponsors first."

"Papa's planning to race again?" Minna suddenly felt as if her heart were filled with sunlight. "I can't tell you how happy that makes me."

"If you're happy, I'm happy." Evan's eyes crinkled at the edges as he smiled. "Your father and Mr. Bartholomew just sat down to a game of chess, so I came to see if there is anything I can do to help you pack."

She gestured toward her shelf. "I may need a cardboard box for my books."

He did a double take when he recognized the faded paper dragon. "I can't believe you kept that after all these years."

"You made such an impression, I didn't want to forget you."

Moments later, the dragon took flight and circled the room before landing on Minna's outstretched hand. She tucked it into the trunk as she slid Evan an affectionate glance. "I wish I'd given you something to remember me by."

"You gave me something far better than a paper dragon." Evan tapped his cheek. "An unforgettable kiss for luck." He took her into his arms. "I told your father I planned to marry you one day."

Minna's eyes widened. "How did he react?"

"He said if I broke your heart, he'd hunt me down and rip me into pieces."

She sighed in relief. "Oh, good."

Evan looked at her askance. "What?"

"I thought he was going to say *no*."

Beast came trotting into the room, looking for attention. As he watched the humans kiss, he wagged his tail in approval.

The End

SNEAK PEEK AT ROYAL PROMENADE

When Alice takes her place as the Princess of Colossus, she's thrust into the world of the Royal Promenade—a reality show in which the kingdom's elite find matches for their sons and daughters. Blade, the fair-haired wizard who makes hearts flutter, and ruggedly handsome Kellan, an elite Ranger with His Majesty's Special Forces, will vie for her hand in marriage. Although the Promenade is filled with excitement, conflict, and glamour, nothing is what it seems. In the end, will Alice be able marry the man she truly loves or will secret plots and intrigue destroy her?

Keep reading for a sneak peek...

EXCERPT FROM ROYAL PROMENADE

When Alice emerged from her suite the following morning, a familiar darkly handsome man in a Ranger uniform was waiting for her in the hallway. Perhaps her stars weren't entirely unlucky after all.

"Oh, hello." She felt a flush of pleasure. "It's nice to see you again."

The man sketched a formal bow. "Ranger Kellan Stratford, at your service."

"I'm Alice Holland." She glanced up and down the corridor. "Where are my guards?"

"Rangers have been assigned to you from now on."

"Is that so?" Her smile slipped. Apparently, Blade had reported her to her father and her security detail had been tightened as a result. "Well, I'm late for my morning at the Minfo."

"Don't mind me. I can keep up."

If Blade thought he could clip her wings by assigning a Ranger to dog her footsteps, she would prove him very wrong indeed.

"That sounds almost like a challenge." Alice gave the man an appraising glance. "Well, then, let's see what you're made of."

She darted off down the hall, descended the marble staircase as if pursued by a pack of devils, and sped from the castle at top speed. With her hair flying like a flag, she sprinted through the garden and into the labyrinth, emerging on the far side in short order. Although she didn't hear Kellan's footfall, she increased her pace nevertheless until she reached the Minfo building. As she reached for the door handle, however, the Ranger beat her to it. He held the door open and made a gesture of invitation. "After you."

"How did you..?" She peered at him, stunned. No sweat prickled at his forehead and his breathing was normal. "Are you a wizard?"

Kellan chuckled. "I'm a Ranger, Princess."

She passed into the lobby, only to discover he was following her. "My other guards always waited outside for me."

"My orders are different."

"Of course they are." Alice strode toward the platinum elevator, pausing when Kellan fell into step beside her. "Must you stay so close?"

"I do."

Alice bit back a sharp retort.

About the Author

Originally from Southern California, Suzanne G. Rogers currently resides in beautiful Savannah, Georgia. She lives on an island populated by exotic birds, deer, otters, and gators.

ALSO BY SUZANNE G. ROGERS

FANTASY

<u>Standalone Titles</u>

Something Wicked in L.A.

Clash of Wills

*The Dragon Rider's Daughter**

Dani & the Immortals

Magical Misperception

Tournament of Chance: Dragon Rebel

*Whimsical Tendencies**

Royal Promenade

<u>The Yden Series</u>

The Last Great Wizard of Yden (Book One)

Dragon Clan of Yden (Book Two)

Secrets of Yden (Book Three)

Kira (Prequel to the Yden Trilogy)

*Available in audiobook format

ALSO BY SUZANNE G. ROGERS

HISTORICAL ROMANCE

<u>The Beaucroft Girls Series</u>

Ruse & Romance (Book One)*

Rake & Romance (Book Two)*

<u>Graceling Hall Series</u>

Larken (Book One)*

Lord Apollo & the Colleen (Book Two)

The Vanishing Beauty (Book Three)

<u>The Gilded Age Series</u>

Duke of a Gilded Age (Book One)

Lady of a Gilded Age (Book Two)

<u>The Mannequin Series</u>

The Mannequin (Book One)*

Grace Unmasked (Book Two)

The Star-Crossed Seamstress (Book Three)

A Chance of Rayne (Book Four)

The Substitute (Book Five)

<u>Standalone Titles</u>

*Jessamine's Folly**

*The Ice Captain's Daughter**

*My Fair Guardian**

Lady Fallows' Secrets

*Spinster**

A Gift for Fiona

An American in Paris of the West

Rumer Has It

The Glass Heart

One Little Kiss

The Prettier Sister

Courtship on Eaton Square

*Available in audiobook format